The Wayfaring Mission

Frances Morlen

The Wayfaring Mission

Histria Christian

Las Vegas ♦ Chicago ♦ Palm Beach

Published in the United States of America by
Histria Books
7181 N. Hualapai Way, Ste. 130-86
Las Vegas, NV 89166 U.S.A.
HistriaBooks.com

Histria Christian is an imprint of Histria Books dedicated to books that embody and promote Christian values and an understanding of the Christian faith. Titles published under the imprints of Histria Books are distributed worldwide.

ISBN 978-1-63213-462-2 (softbound)
ISBN 978-1-63213-463-9 (eBook)

Chapter 1

An acrid gust alarmed Ellen's senses, as she stepped through the Mission's heavy wooden doors into the chill of early March, at 9,000 feet. The icy mountain mixture tingled with melting snow, crisp, pungent pines, junipers, and yes, smoke. It was the bane of the high desert mountains of the Lincoln National Forest in New Mexico. Over the northern peaks that surrounded the secluded valley where Wayfaring Mission lay sheltered, a column of smoke rose as ominous as the ancient warning signals of bygone days. The media perpetually updating the sweeping destruction were not predicting that the fire would reach the valley, but experience had taught her how volatile the March winds could be. Wind gusts of thirty to forty miles per hour could rapidly create a raging inferno.

Her tensed muscles jumped slightly when Char, her large German shepherd, nuzzled her hand and lifted his head to the smell of the drifting smoke. Named for the similarity of his coat color to the charred stumps, he also had experience testing the wind, and she watched him closely for signs of undue agitation. Had not Saint Francis encouraged goodwill and brotherhood with all the living creatures? She certainly felt in need of a brother, as her eyes scanned the blackened scarred mountainside where the flames had raced through the wooded peaks during last year's fire season. Miraculously, although the scorched scars raked the mountainsides, the valley had been spared. That sense of protected space was one of the many reasons she had fallen in love with this place. The high elevation allowed more moisture than most of this dry region of the desert southwest; this valley remained lush with green during the summer months or blanketed with snow, as it was now, throughout the winter. Entering the valley was like climbing from the parched desert into a hidden oasis where lofty pines stood guard around the perimeter.

The old mission that Ellen had converted into an inn embodied peace and permanence as it sat nestled in the southern end of the valley. She remembered that the last time the fires had threatened; a small procession of elderly women, descendants possibly from the earliest Spanish land grant families, had made their way to the chapel to pray for protection. They filed in, their starched black dresses rustling with lacy white prayer shawls over their heads, like spirits from a departed age. At least one small bowed figure knelt before the altar day and night until, as if by the sheer force of their faith, the flames were extinguished. Ellen was not Roman Catholic, but she could never lock the massive doors of the adobe chapel to anyone of faith.

Franciscan friars had first built the Mission as an outpost in the 1700s to evangelize the fierce Mescalero Apaches. Recognizing the unique refuge character of the surroundings, they had carved a portion of Jeremiah 9:2 into the expansive beam that crossed the Chapel. "Oh, that I had in the wilderness a lodging place of wayfaring men." It had become her secluded haven for the past two years. When her husband, Dr. Martin Wright, a wandering academic, had not returned from his last remote destination, it was as if her sense of security had gone with him. Eventually, when the word finally came that his plane had crashed with no survivors, she had desperately needed to retreat from the world, even from her adult children. They were on the threshold of life; they did not need her hanging around as a haunting caricature of loss. After the memorial service, she had started driving; fleeing actually, toward the mountains escaping the heat, the chaos, the questions, and the uncertainty.

No one wanted to believe that he was only a professor. What was he doing there? As if she knew now or had ever known, what drew him to the places that he went. At some point, she had stopped asking since the answer never came. The only assurances he had ever given was his activities were not political, there was no other woman, and although he truly loved her, he felt compelled to go.

Within the sheltering walls of the Mission, she had settled into a routine that allowed her to feel that he was really not dead, just away traveling, like so many other times. His extensive library was there with memorabilia from his travels decorating every available space. It was all that remained to give her a sense of his presence still with her. She made it accessible to the other world-weary guests who seemed to find their way to the Wayfaring Mission. Although there was satellite media and internet available, the connections were situated in a room well away from the central living areas, so as not to intrude on the environment of quiet tranquility. She no longer wanted to know what happened outside the valley. Except for the fires.

The Mission layout was a large square with a central courtyard. Walls of thick red-brown adobe with small wrought iron worked openings protected the outside walls of the structures. From the exterior, everything appeared smooth and rounded without sharp edges and harsh corners as if the strong arms of the Mission embraced the inhabitants. The double-thick walls of the adobe chapel with its ornately carved wood and stone crucifix comprised one section of the wall. The old refectory now held the kitchen and dining area followed by the only two-story buildings in the Mission; the great room, and the library.

In the rounded front corner of the square, filling what used to be a storage area was Ellen's office. She loved it for the deep-set windows with their wrought iron-work allowing her to see both the gravel driveway to the entrance and from the other window a view of the expansive green valley enclosed in the rugged arms of the mountains. The office also held a narrow hidden circular staircase leading up to her apartment above the library. At the other end of her apartment was a small balcony that looked out over the two-storied open great room with its immense wooden beams lifting the space. The office also had a door leading to the court-yard, which allowed Ellen easy access to greet her guests as they came through the arched entrance with its heavy, intricately carved wooden doors embedded with turquoise accents.

On the other side of the entry were her cook and caretaker, Rosita and Manuel's, living quarters and the area that once held the stables. Now there were only four horses left, and so the rest of the closed-door stalls held a variety of gardening equipment and recreational vehicles. The final section connecting to the chapel wall included the media room and the cells where the monks had once lived which she had converted into sleeping quarters and restrooms for her guests.

Around the interior walls ran a corridor fronted with arched pillars, containing a patio courtyard with a stone-carved fountain that flowed year-round from a pure underground spring. The Friars had chosen well when they decided on the location. Two huge trees offered summer shade when the rest of the courtyard would transform in the desert sun to a kaleidoscope of color in the peaceful garden retreat lovingly tended by Manuel.

Ellen turned from her surveillance of the drifting smoke as a wrinkled, worn hand patted her arm reassuringly. Rosita was passing by on her way to begin dinner. Although Ellen's Spanish was limited, this was not a problem since; Manuel, in particular, had learned English as well as other languages, from a succession of monks of various nationalities. When the last of the monks passed away, the couple had remained to care for the Mission until the diocese had sold her the valuable property.

Ellen could not imagine ever asking them to leave their small home set in the thick adobe walls. They belonged to the Mission; as if, having come years ago as a newly married couple they had imbibed the spirit of the place so thoroughly, that to remove them would require separation of the soul from the body. They sometimes looked at her with curious compassion, but they had never pried or asked her for details of her life. While Manuel continued to perform the offices of deacon at the small chapel, Ellen wondered how officially sanctioned his activities were when he greeted the faithful collection of little old ladies each Sunday.

It was her policy never to book her guests for less than a week at a time. She found that lessened the upset to the daily routine and gave Wayfaring Mission a more peaceful settled atmosphere. This week there were not many guests staying in the simple rooms that once were cells for Franciscan monks. Stephan Pierce, a tall, thin graying writer with a thoughtful face and a faint British accent. A young artist named Heather with a somewhat haunted look in her eyes, who claimed she only wanted a place to paint undisturbed but had the fearful hunted look of someone hiding. James Ring was a handsome young musician who requested a spare room to compose his music. Jack Smith, a middle-aged man, had a hard-lined face and a military haircut. The Johnsons were a big city Texas corporate couple who said that they wanted one last ski trip before the season ended, though apparently, not prepared for the more rustic accommodations, they had spent most of this first day in the media room pecking furiously at their computers. There were no children this week, although Ellen welcomed children.

After dinner, the guests wandered into the large, great room full of burnished hardwood, and soft leathers accented with colorful Native American blankets and patterns. Manuel had laid a fire in the massive stone fireplace, which opened on one side into the great room and on the other into the library providing warmth and light for spirit and body. Lounging in the supple leather chairs, they sipped coffee or Rosita's smooth dark Mexican hot chocolate. Manuel picked up his antique-looking guitar and began softly strumming enchanting Spanish rhythms. Heather, sitting with her notebook in a corner, was surreptitiously sketching

James, who was drinking in the music and watching Stephan fill an intricately carved pipe.

Ellen hated cigarettes and despised cigars, but the smell of pipe tobacco often reminded her of the incense she and Martin had encountered on a trip to India. Feeling it was somewhat self-indulgent, she had made him ask the permission of the other guests before he lighted it. Jack Smith alone did not seem engaged in the setting but sat watching her over the edge of his coffee cup.

"Does he never leave your side?" he asked. The hard edge to his voice made his question sound more like an accusation. He gestured toward Ellen as she stood with her hand resting on Char's neck.

"Not often." She replied, not appreciating his tone.

"I wouldn't want him too," she added rubbing the furry upturned head. "He's my best friend."

"I thought dogs were supposed to be a *man's* best friend?" He responded with a tinge of sarcasm.

"Maybe Char has better taste." She quipped as she turned away frowning slightly. What was his problem?

Ellen retreated into the library lit only by the flickering fireplace and passed through to the seclusion of her office to see if there was an update on the fires. The news reported that it raged on, not yet contained, but a wind change seemed to be pushing it away from them at the moment. Ellen released the breath she had not realized she was holding, although it was better not to be too hopeful. Char's ears perked up, and he eyed the open door into the library. He did not bark, but his twitching ears were alert aware that someone had entered. She stepped quietly from her office and switched on the closest reading lamp. Stephan, aromatic with the faint slightly sweet, spicy fragrance of his pipe stood in the shadowed doorway. She pressed the panel in her office illumining the library's recessed lighting.

"Please feel free to borrow a book. Just be sure to sign it out at the registry there." She pointed to a leather-bound book lying on a carved wooden monk's desk under the window.

"Aren't you afraid someone will walk away with them?" he asked raising an eyebrow. "Some of these are quite valuable." He gingerly picked up an early version of Paradise Lost with Gustave Dore illustrations.

Ellen shrugged, "My husband always shared his books, although he fretted over them like lost children until they returned." She smiled wistfully at the memory. Stephan was looking at her attentively.

"Your husband is deceased?" He asked with kind curiosity.

Ellen nodded, wanting to avoid a discussion of details and changed the subject.

"I find most guests are interested only in the current best-sellers, not these dusty old things." She said laughed nonchalantly, gesturing around the room.

"Well you may have to search me when I leave, I find them very intriguing," he said seriously. However, when Ellen glanced at him, she found he was examining one of the many pictures of her husband. Afraid of more questions, Ellen locked her office door and returned to her other guests. James was perched on the arm of the chair where Manuel continued to play softly. He seemed to be breathing in the music watching the intricate strumming patterns that seemed to flow so naturally from Manuel's rough fingers. Passing behind Heather's chair, Ellen stopped to admire the impromptu portrait of James that she was intently sketching.

"That is incredible!" she exclaimed with feeling in a low voice so as not to reveal the young woman's secret.

"Thanks, but you do know who that is, don't you?" Heather responded in an intense whisper.

"Um, he's a musician, right?" He had looked vaguely familiar, but Ellen was well aware that she was way out of touch with current pop culture, "That is James Ring, the foremost concert violinist of the past five years!" Heather said triumphantly with shining eyes. Ellen was not aware that concert violinists generally caused this sort of adoration in young women. She was obviously behind the times.

"I need to ask you to please respect his privacy while he is here. He may have come here to escape the spotlight for a while." Ellen asked seriously.

"Are you kidding?" Heather said with an impish grin. "I want him all to myself!"

Ellen smiled sardonically, "Watch out James!" she thought.

Ellen retrieved a tray and began to remove the empty cups scattered around the room interrupting the Johnsons in a heated discussion on whether to gamble or ski the next day. The gist of the conversation indicated that Mr. Johnson might have a bit of a gambling problem. The fact that the Mescalero Apache tribe had placed a casino so conveniently within the range of the ski slopes had not been revealed to Mrs. Johnson when Mr. Johnson selected this location for their vacation. Ellen removed their cups and turned away. As she reached to retrieve Jack's cup, he grasped her wrist.

"How about another cup of coffee?" He demanded in his imperious tone. Ellen realized he was looking past her to Char, who stepped toward him rumbling a warning growl. The cups rattled as she pulled away nearly upsetting the tray she carried.

"No problem, would you like it black or with cream, and sugar?" She asked somewhat icily.

"It would take more than cream and sugar to sweeten me up, don't you think?" he taunted.

Manuel had stopped playing when the dishes clattered and was watching as well. Ellen moved toward the dining room door with Char following. After depositing the cups, she knelt and wrapped her arms around Char.

"Thank you, good dog" She whispered burying her face in his thick fur until her anger and agitation subsided. There was no doubt that she should not be praising her dog for growling at one of her guests, but she did not care.

When she returned with another cup of black coffee, Manuel met her to take it from her and carry it to Jack who could not help noticing with a scornful smirk. Ellen passed on through the great room and library to her office where she shut the door. Char had never growled at anyone. Of course, no one had ever laid a hand on her before. Even now, Char sat staring at the door tense and ready. Why did Jack seem to be deliberately badgering her regarding her dog? Maybe he did not like dogs, or perhaps found her dependence on Char amusing? On the other hand, was he intentionally testing to see how far he could go to provoke either her or her dog?

Ellen retrieved his registration from her computer. Who was this guy, and why had he come? She had thought that maybe he was a military man who needed a holiday. His record said he was interested in skiing and hiking. Ellen told herself to relax. Some people got pleasure from aggravating others; that's all. She would need to keep out of arms reach, literally. She was not worried about being physically attractive to anyone. At fifty plus, she recognized she was no beauty, and she dressed for comfort, not for style or attraction. Still, she was not accustomed to being handled roughly by a man. Whatever his shortcomings, her husband had always treated her with respect and gentleness and had demanded the same from their sons.

Bless Manuel's heart! He had raised Char's mother when an eastern orthodox monk had brought her to the Mission from New Skete, world-renowned for its German shepherd breeding and training program. Char had been a two-year-old when Ellen arrived, and Manuel had immediately given her this well-trained, obedient, and loyal friend. Manuel was probably the only other person who understood how extraordinary Char's actions had been. Undoubtedly, he had been alarmed. Glancing out of her office before locking the door, she could only see Stephan sitting by a lamp absorbed in some dusty volume.

Ellen suddenly felt tired. Unlocking the rounded wooden door that appeared to be a closet at the back of her office, she climbed the stairs hidden within to her small apartment. At such times, it was difficult not to question the wisdom of choosing to work in a public service industry. The ever-present requirement to meet, not only the needs, but also the wants of her guests was demanding. It overwhelmed her now and then, but she was afraid if she ever retreated, she would never return. Someone would discover her fossilized remains in a remote cabin somewhere. Staying engaged in life since Martin's disappearance had become more a matter of discipline than desire. Activity could suggest a life with purpose.

Ellen did not turn on a light but stepped toward her balcony that overlooked the great room. She had left one of the doors open and in the darkness could discreetly hear and see what went on below. Apparently, the Johnson's discussion had become a full-scale argument that culminated in Mrs. Johnson stomping angrily from the room. James was attentively listening to Manuel explain a particular fingering technique. Heather had moved closer, appearing it seemed, to be incredibly interested.

Where was Jack? When Ellen did discover him, he was looking up directly into her eyes. Alarmed, she stumbled backward further into the room. As her children would say, this guy was creeping her out! Moving to the other side of her small sitting room, she found that he had also moved out of sight. Since Manuel was looking toward the library, Ellen crept silently back down the stairs to her office placing her ear close to the door. Her blood chilled when she heard the click of someone testing the heavy iron latch. She laid her hand against Char's chest to keep him quiet as the hair on the back of his neck began to rise.

"Did you need to speak with Ellen?" Stephan's voice filtered faintly through the gap under the door. Ellen knelt in front of the door bending down to hear better. "I believe she may have retired." He mentioned, casually turning a page without lifting his eyes to the intruder.

"What are you doing in here?" Jack asked aggressively in his demanding way stepping back away from the door.

"I would appear to be reading," Stephan said in a bored voice. "Not that it is any concern of yours. Ellen allows guests to borrow volumes from the library, or you could always go to the media room if you find reading too strenuous." He suggested dryly.

Ignoring or oblivious to his sarcasm, Jack continued his questioning, "Is this her husband?" He asked gesturing to a photograph of a small white-bearded man in front of an ancient Buddhist temple.

"I believe it was; she said he was deceased," Stephan answered indifferently.

Jack continued around the room carefully scrutinizing each photo.

"He seems to have traveled a lot." From behind the door, Ellen wondered why everything the man said sounded like an accusation.

"Indeed," was Stephan's slightly bored response.

"Where was he when he died?" Jack persisted. Ellen noticed he did not ask how her husband had died.

"I did not ask. I did not wish to pry." Stephan responded in a slightly aggravated tone.

"You Brits just ain't got no curiosity, do you?" Jack jeered.

"I mind my own business, and I suggest you do the same," Stephan said firmly.

"And if I don't?" came the belligerent reply.

The question hung in the air. Stephan did not answer, and after muttering something derogatory which Ellen could not hear, Jack stalked from the room. She leaned back against her desk rubbing the ache in her neck with one hand. In the two years since opening Wayfaring Mission, she had encountered her share of troubles from problematic guests, but there had been relief in finally escaping the questions about Martin. Now, this Jack seemed determined to rake through her personal life. Time was supposed to heal, and yet even after two years, her heart still felt raw and wounded whenever he came to mind.

Ellen could not bear to, and yet could not avoid, thinking about Martin's death. Imagining her husband's plane crashing in a ball of fire was her re-occurring nightmare. What did it matter now, where he was when he died? He had always maintained that people needed access to education for themselves and their children. If because of their belief in God they were denied the opportunity for education, then he would bring it to them. Ellen had admired his faith and conviction, even if the separations had strained their marriage and family life. It was his calling, and she could not deny him that. Somehow, she had always managed to muddle through with the children until he returned. Then inevitably, the house would fill with students and philosophical, and faith discussions would swirl for days until he was off again. The number of students who had come to her at the memorial service to express their gratitude had overwhelmed her. Many told how Martin had helped them to find faith in God or, at least, encouraged them to begin searching.

God had seemed so real to her when Martin was alive. She had prayerfully and daily depended on God for wisdom while raising her children. The times of counseling and guiding students to the knowledge of God and relationship with Him had been incredibly rewarding. However, when Martin did not return, it was if she had entered a dark void. God was out there somewhere, but she could not find Him, and she did not know what to say to Him anymore. Of course, there were myriads of "why" questions that swarmed like angry bees for the first few months. There just seemed to be no answers, so she had stopped asking. Instead, she had come to the Mission and had found a modicum of stability, if not peace. Within these solid shielding walls, she had been trying to escape, not only the questions from without but also those from within her own heart.

Ellen jumped at the jingle of the small bell outside her office door that led to the inner courtyard. Manuel entered to give her his nightly report. After reviewing his list of necessary supplies and repairs, which Ellen never disputed, they discussed the fire danger and precautions. Finishing with the business of the day, Manuel bent down and looked for a long minute into Char's black eyes while rubbing his hands gently over him as if examining him. He whispered something quietly in Spanish to which Char thumped his tail softly. When Manuel stood, his face was serious, but still maintained its calm strength.

"Has he ever growled at someone before?" Ellen asked quietly.

"No, he has not," Manuel replied firmly. "He has, however, growled when there was a rattlesnake close by."

In the look that passed between them, Ellen felt she had all the confirmation that she needed regarding Mr. Smith's potential danger. Manuel patted her arm gently and slipped out the door into the darkened courtyard. After securely locking the office doors, Ellen trudged wearily up the steps to her apartment. Through the slightly opened balcony door, she could see Manuel turning off the main lights in the great room. He paused at the library door to speak to Stephan, and Ellen could catch the faint pleasant odor of the pipe smoke; although their voices were too soft to understand the exchange. After a moment of internal debate, she decided to close and lock the balcony door for the very first time.

Her sleep was restless; filled with dreams of hands reaching for her. Nightmares had been a problem since Martin's death; consequently, Ellen had learned to force herself into consciousness when they overwhelmed her. The struggle between outward acceptance, even healing, and inward despair continued. Tonight, she slept lightly; since Char prowled discontentedly in front of the closed balcony doors where he usually slept. Even when she finally gave up and opened the doors for him; he could not seem to settle.

Chapter 2

In spite of her disturbed sleep, Ellen woke early as she always did, anxious to get a steaming cup of strong coffee from Rosita. Passing back through the library, with the faint aroma of Stephan's pipe still hanging in the air, she had a vague feeling that something was out of place. Postponing investigating, she hurried to check on the fire's progress which seemed to be moving inexorably toward the ski slope access road. Ellen wondered if the Johnsons would leave or head to the casino. The others were not a concern since skiing did not seem to be on their agenda. Except for Jack, whose real agenda remained a mystery.

Ellen left her office and opened the heavy doors to let Char outside the Mission walls for his morning walk. The sharp chill of the mountain air was invigorating as was the ever-present tangy breath of the pines. The spiraling flight of a raven drew her eyes with apprehension out over the valley toward the mountains venting their streamers of smoke. Foreboding heightened her awareness, and she felt, rather than heard, someone behind her.

"Is it headed this direction?" Jack spoke gruffly.

She jerked slightly at his voice, as did Char who turned quickly and loped to her side.

"Not at the moment, although they may close some of the roads to the slopes, so I hope you weren't planning on skiing today," Ellen informed him, keeping her voice deliberately steady.

"No, I think I will just hang around here today and relax. Maybe do some hiking," Jack answered nonchalantly.

"Good idea, there are some great trails and the snow is not too deep now," Ellen reassured him reluctantly while her heart sank.

The last thing she needed was to have to deal with him all day. While leading the way toward the dining room, Ellen noticed the hackles along Char's neck had stiffened, and although he did not growl, his suspicion of Jack was undeniable. Some men were just not safe to turn your back on. Ellen was pretty sure the hair on the back of her neck was standing up too as Jack followed her down the corridor.

Inside the dining room, she found Heather had managed to join James at his breakfast table, and he motioned to her as she passed.

"Excuse me Ellen, but is the chapel locked? I was wondering if I could practice there for a couple of hours. I will only play sacred music of course; I just don't want to get rusty while vacationing." He explained eagerly glancing at Heather, "Heather thought she might like to do some sketches of the interior and the crucifix." Ellen smiled warmly at the young people. Nice move Heather.

"Of course, we keep it unlocked through most of the day. Manuel opens it early for his observation of Matins." They thanked her, and Ellen moved away relieved that they would be occupied.

Stephan was reading as he enjoyed his tea and toast. He had been quite pleased to see the selection of oriental teas that were available, asking her how she managed to get them here. Ellen smiled wistfully thinking of the Asian students who sent them almost as memorials to Martin. It was always lovely and yet painful to receive the packages with their addresses that seemed to come not from foreign lands, but from far away former days. It was almost too much for her to drink them herself. The aroma and taste brought her back to the moments when circles of smiling students eagerly leaned forward to catch the words of the professor sitting cross-legged on the floor in front of them. Stephan heard the sadness when she explained that they were gifts from friends of her husband.

"He seems to have had friends from a lot of countries." Cut in Jack who apparently had been eavesdropping and now rose to look at the labels on the tea tray.

"China, Sri Lanka, India, even African Rooibos tea." He read as he scanned the intricately decorated containers.

Ellen wondered why everything he said sounded like an accusation.

"Yes, he traveled quite extensively for his work." She answered matter-of-factly, as she moved away.

She managed to make it to the kitchen door and to slip through pretending not to hear his query regarding exactly what sort of work her husband had done.

Inside the kitchen, she leaned wearily against the counter before reaching into the cupboard for Char's food and dish. Rosita gently placed a chair behind her and pressed her into the seat. Grinning conspiratorially, she handed Ellen a churro that had somehow avoided the morning menu and her coffee. Ellen smiled, more grateful for her motherly concern than for the treat. When she rose to finish attending to breakfast, Rosita placed a firm restraining hand on her shoulder and said Manuel would take care of things.

Feeling a cowardly relief, Ellen slipped out of the kitchen and walked down the arched corridor to her office, subconsciously quickening her pace past the dining room door. After rechecking the inevitable road closures, she returned to find the Johnsons and inform them that access road to the ski slope had been closed by the forest service until the fire danger was passed. While the slopes themselves still had snowpack, the road leading there through the wooded lower elevations was definitely in harm's way. Locating them in the dining room, she relayed the information. Mrs. Johnson at once huffed off to pack her bags demanding reimbursement and threatening legal recriminations. Upon her departure, Mr. Johnson gleefully announced that he would not be leaving with his wife. Ellen was secretly relieved that her guests always paid in advance. She was less worried about reimbursing Mrs. Johnson than she would have been getting any remaining money from Mr. Johnson when he was through at the casino.

Ellen was pleased that Jack appeared to have gone on his hike. She hoped he had informed Manuel where he intended to go since it was easy to get disoriented in the mountains without a guide. As she entered the library, she came to a stop when she saw Stephan slip an intricately decorated black lacquer box back on a shelf while hastily picking up a book lying on the table. Ellen knew the box was empty, so his furtive action surprised her. With a sheepish look, Stephan explained, "I thought I had seen this type of black lacquer before. Is it from Myanmar? Cambodia?" Ellen thought he looked guilty. Was he planning to steal it or something?

"I believe it came from Burma or Myanmar if you prefer. Have you been there?" Ellen inquired searching for a reason for his discomfort.

"I have not, but I was sent a box like this from a friend once. He never told me where it came from, just curious." Stephan spoke rapidly, embarrassed.

Maybe she imagined that Stephan had looked toward Martin's picture when he had said "friend." She glanced slowly around the room taking a mental inventory. Everything seemed to be in order. Casually, she walked to the checkout table and glanced at the registry. The only book listed was Martin's favorite copy of Don Quixote. He had always laughingly referred to Don Quixote as his patron saint; given their similar tendencies to fight futile battles with imaginary enemies that turn out to be windmills.

"So, you like Don Quixote?" she asked without glancing up.

"Of course, he's the patron saint of lost causes, isn't he?" Stephan inquired softly.

A chill crept up Ellen's spine.

"That is what my husband always said." She said somewhat haltingly. Her blood froze when he replied, "I know."

"How would you know what my husband said? She asked with apprehension.

"It is because I knew your husband, that I came here. It was vital that I find you. I must talk to you soon!" Stephan spoke quietly but with intensity.

Ellen sank into the chair as her legs went weak. Char leaned against her leg and whined. She did not even realize that Stephan had left the room until he pressed a glass of water into her hand moments later. Sipping it automatically, gradually regaining her voice, "How did you?" she began, but Stephan quieted her with his hand. Jack had stepped into the doorway.

"There you are!" he stopped suddenly looking from one to the other with accusing inquiry.

"I want to rent one of the 4-wheelers, and I can't find Manuel!" His eyes were full of suspicion when Stephan answered calmly instead of Ellen, "He went to listen to James playing his violin in the chapel, I believe."

Finding no way to prolong the conversation, Jack turned on his heel and stalked out the door. Ellen once more opened her mouth to speak, and again Stephan cautioned her.

"Let's step into your office if you don't mind."

Feeling the initial shock beginning to subside, Ellen brushed off his proffered hand and moved reluctantly into her office. Char whined softly and pressed against her side as she sank into her office chair. Her mind was slowly beginning to produce rational thoughts. It was not so strange that Stephan would have met her husband. Martin had friends and contacts around the world. There was nothing extraordinary about it. Except that, not one of them had ever made their way here. No one from that life had ever come to find her. Ellen saw Stephan now with a distrust bordering on animosity, which only increased when Stephan shut and locked the office door.

"May I?" Stephan asked gently motioning to the leather armchair that Ellen used for visitors. Ellen gestured angrily now toward the seat and him.

"Why are you here? How did you find me, and what do you want?" She demanded coldly. The numbness was gone, and so were the careful restraints she normally placed on herself. Her eyes were flashing, and her hand trembled as she gestured toward him.

"I did not come here to upset you. I should have found a better way to introduce myself, I guess. I did not understand that you wanted to remain concealed." His tone was gentle, placating. Leaning forward earnestly he continued, "You did not change your name, and Martin often talked about these mountains. I drew my own conclusions and looked for you here." The way he spoke of Martin with such familiarity seemed to open some vulnerable hidden place in Ellen's inner being. When she spoke, her voice sounded raw and wounded.

"Why should I have to change my name to be left alone? Why did you need to find me?"

"I just wanted to ask you a couple of questions." He answered.

A cry of disgust and anger tore from Ellen's throat that was both a sob and groan. All the unanswerable questions were the reason she had escaped to the Mission in the first place. What difference could it possibly make now where Martin was going or what he had been doing? Why couldn't they leave her dead husband to rest in peace?

"Who are you, and what gives you the right to ask me questions?" She rasped with painful accusation. "My husband is dead, and I am done answering pointless questions! There are no more answers!"

She had wrenched herself from her seat and reached the door when she felt Stephan's hand laid gently on her shoulder.

"Please!" he pleaded softly. "I am so sorry that I upset you! I did not realize you did not want to be found. Please, let me explain!"

Ellen turned her back on him and went to the deep-set window that looked out over the valley. She clung to the delicately curved iron bars feeling exposed; her sanctuary was gone. Wayfaring Mission could no longer be her hiding place, her refuge. Fear and despair crept toward her like an avalanche beginning at the top of the mountain, and there was nowhere to run.

Wearily, she sank into her chair where Char licked her hand and whined his concern.

"Go ahead." She sighed dropping her face in her trembling hands.

"I was one of his supporters. I'm one of the ones who sent him, or who set up meetings for him." He spoke it like a confession and dropped his eyes at the look Ellen gave him.

She had never met most of the elusive people who paid Martin's salary and like benevolent puppet masters had manipulated not just her husband, but also her life from afar. Of course, none of them knew the hardship his absence, and finally, his death had caused; they only saw the work he was accomplishing and his noble sacrifice. Now that she was facing one of them, Ellen wondered if she hated him.

"I believed in what he was doing! No one else could go in and out of those countries and accomplish what Martin did without compromising either himself or our contacts. He gave people not just education or aid; he gave them the hope of the gospel! He was a light in some very dark places." The urgency in his voice trailed off sadly.

It was not that Ellen had ever doubted that the words were true. She had even characterized her husband as a modern-day apostle Paul. It was just that he spent all his effort and attention courageously on the ministry out there, and even when he was home, there were students and others who took whatever remained of his focus and energy. Perhaps that was why the ancient apostle had advocated the single life. Ellen looked at the man regarding her with sad consternation. Was it his fault? Did he help cause Martin's death, or was he simply a tool that enabled Martin to live out a calling he felt God compelling him to fulfill. Who was to blame, and did it even matter? She heard the dread in her voice asking, "What do you want to know?"

Stephan straightened in his chair and leaned forward eagerly. "Do you have any idea where he was going, what city?"

Why did they ask her that question? It came to her now as a repeating nightmare, and her answer came with just as much horrendous certainty.

"For some reason, he never gave me his itinerary. I guess he thought it was safer that way! I only ever had his flight schedule. The last flight on his schedule is the one that they found burning pieces of scattered all over the mountain!" She spoke harshly. Stephan's response paralyzed her in her seat.

"But what if he wasn't on that flight?" he asked with guarded intensity. "What if he had already been detained or captured before he reached that city?" Ellen realized she had been holding her breath and let it out in a gasp.

"No! He was on the list of passengers on that flight! Besides, he would have found a way to contact me if he missed his flight or was delayed! He always did!" She spoke shaking with frustrated anger.

She could not go through this again! Without his body to bury, acceptance of the inevitable had been difficult. For months after the crash, she had hoped that in some way he had been spared. Wishing, hoping and praying, that somehow he would contact her or come home. Resignation and despair had replaced hope long ago. There was no way!

"Besides, if he was abducted for ransom, why were there no demands? If he had been taken hostage to make a political or radical religious statement, he would have quickly been recorded either alive or while being assassinated, and they would have posted it for the extremists viewing pleasure. There has been nothing. For two years- nothing!" Ellen's voice poured out her pain and bitterness. She had been through this all before; it was pointless to continue. However, the next information was new.

"Did you know that Jack Smith works for the state department? We are not certain which branch sent him. We think they have discovered something about Martin's location, and they sent Jack to find out if it would be worth their efforts to get involved. In other words, is the information that Martin has valuable enough for them to reveal his whereabouts?" Stephan spoke urgently, leaning forward.

Ellen sat dumbly for a moment, realizing that he had just referred to Martin in the present tense. Who was this, "we", and why would Martin have any valuable information that anyone in the government would want?

"Wait, you think he was taken captive and is being held somewhere? If Mr. Smith knows where he is then why is he here?" she asked incredulously.

He continued, "I cannot tell you why he is here. The problem is how do we find out from Jack what they know? They won't risk the resources to get Martin out! Our only hope is to find him and to attempt to rescue him through our opposition military contacts. Even though the probability of finding him is small, we must try; the situation with this terrorist group is becoming more volatile every day." He pleaded for her understanding.

Ellen felt as if a giant hand was squeezing her chest. She could not do this! Whatever delusion Stephan wanted to pull her into, she knew that believing him would eventually mean losing Martin all over again. Even if he were alive and held captive somewhere, it would be impossible to get that information from Jack! He was a professional at keeping secrets if what Stephan said was true. Impatiently, she reached for the door to the courtyard and wrenched it open. She turned her face away as she waited for him to leave. Sadly, Stephan slipped through the door without protest. On the step, he turned to look into her agonized face, "I have handled this so poorly," he murmured with sincere contrition, "I hope someday you will be able to forgive me. I guess I was only thinking of the slim chance of finding him. I did not consider the effect this would have on you. I should never have mentioned it until I had concrete proof." He bowed slightly and turned away.

Ellen did not look at him but lifted tear-filled eyes to the hills beyond the walls of the Mission. The smoke was there, and vaguely she registered that it seemed to be growing. It did not matter anymore. She could not stay here. It was no longer her refuge. They, Stephan and this agent Jack, had violated her sanctuary; exposing her hiding place. There was no way that Martin could still be alive. Stephan would raise her expectations only to dash them against the rubble of all her former false hopes. Ellen turned aimlessly and stumbled down the corridor toward the chapel. Pushing open the heavy wooden door, she sensed, almost more than heard, the music. It seemed to filter through her fevered consciousness like a cooling vapor.

James was standing in the center aisle near the altar swaying with the music as if he and his instrument were one being. His eyes were closed, and although he was playing softly, the acoustics expanded the music until it enveloped the room. Ellen slipped unnoticed into the side of one of the back pews.

"Our Father, which art in heaven," the violin sang with reverence and assurance.

She had known Him that way at one time. Ever since she was a child growing up in the home of a pastor of a small country church, she had believed in God. Given the strictness of her upbringing, God as Father to her was a, sometimes, harsh disciplinarian, but He was still one who could be entreated, who showed love by providing and protecting. She had only ever wanted to please Him.

"Thy kingdom come, thy will be done," swelled in the second strain.

That was what so many well-intentioned comforters had said when Martin disappeared; that and "the Lord gives and takes away, blessed be the name of the Lord." The ones who had glibly advocated that mantra; had rarely had to say it themselves. Like Job's comforters, they judged her suffering as if it should be a privilege to have her husband die while doing "the Lord's work".

"Forgive us our debts, as we forgive our debtors," pleaded the voice of the violin.

Maybe she could not be forgiven because she could not forgive. Her list seemed to be growing longer. There was Jack, who harassed and questioned; Stephan and the others, who sent Martin and enabled him were difficult to forgive. But they were nothing compared to the challenge of forgiving Martin for choosing this life of separation from her and his children, and hardest of all God, for requiring him to do so.

"Lead us not into temptation, but deliver us from evil," the petition continued.

Her temptation was to run, to hide, to give it all up, and to disappear permanently. What was the evil? Was it Jack with his interrogation and accusations? She had been through it all before when she was reeling with shock and grief; how much worse could it get now that she was numb? Was the evil the false hope that Stephan's calm assurance wanted to give? Hope that raised itself with strength like the snowcapped mountains but could come roaring down with an avalanche of despair. Was Martin still out there in the clutches of evil men awaiting rescue? Maybe he was waiting to be delivered from them. Two years of trauma reminded her where that track of thinking would take her imagination, for her sanity's sake she could not let herself go there.

The last swelling strains of "thine is the kingdom and the power and the glory forever, amen" poured from the instrument filling the air surrounding her. She felt like an exile from that kingdom, as if somehow when Martin died, the gates had closed and for the first time she was on the outside. She did not recognize the landscape around her. She must be lost. She did not realize that she had bent over in the pew clutching her arms around her knees; as if to hold herself together until she felt Manuel's gentle hand on her shoulder.

At the sight of her ashen tear-stained face, he gently reached out and cupped her cheek in his worn hand.

"Oh mija, I am so sorry!" he said tenderly as to a small child. Ellen struggled to smile wanly and rose unsteadily to her feet. She was grateful that as usual Manuel did not ask for an explanation, but moved forward to speak to Andrew and Heather allowing her to slip unnoticed from the chapel. Char, who had waited outside the chapel door, moved quickly to her side when she faltered dizzily at the door. Ellen leaned on him momentarily before making her way down the corridor to her office.

Chapter 3

Automatically switching on her computer, Ellen checked the fire status. The fires were momentarily under control, but high wind advisories did not bode well. Under normal circumstances, she would have been agitated and concerned, but now Ellen just felt detached. What did it matter? She locked her office doors and trudged up the stairs to her rooms. At the top of the stairs, Char lifted his nose and began moving cautiously around the room sniffing. Several places he stopped and the hair on his neck rose. Finally, he stood frozen in front of the large oak desk where she kept her private papers. Ellen began frantically opening drawers; it was immediately evident that someone had gone through her papers. Who could have done it? Was it Jack or Stephan? If Jack had been in the room, that would explain Char's behavior; he had never reacted that way when around Stephan. Pawing frantically through her files, she realized that only her file containing information regarding Martin's death was missing. Jack must have searched her room while she was in the chapel!

White hot outrage and a sense of violation burned within her. It was not as if she even had anything to hide from either state informers or concerned supporters. It was just that those few scraps of paper were hers! They were all that remained to detail what she had lost; her fragments that tied her, however tenuously, to the man she had so desperately tried to love! Jack had no right to them, and she would get them back! Ellen slammed the drawers and throwing open the doors to her balcony scanned the great room below. All she saw was a rather forlorn looking Mr. Johnson, slumped in a chair with a magazine. Bounding down the stairs, she caught his somewhat alarmed expression as she rushed past him.

Down in the courtyard, Stephan and Manuel were deep in conversation when Ellen strode rapidly toward them with such fury that they stopped mid-sentence to look at her with apprehension.

"Where is Mr. Smith?" she spat out the words loudly and contemptuously.

"Uh, actually that is what we were discussing. Apparently, Jack did not wait to find Manuel, he hot-wired one of the 4-wheelers and headed up into the mountains." Stephan replied.

"Well that is not all that he's stolen, I think he may have taken some papers from my room!" Ellen spat out watching the e anger that flashed over Manuel's face and the dismay on Stephan's.

"He is a thief! We must find him!" Manuel's face lightened. "Also, there was not much fuel in the machine, and I think he may not have petrol to make it back if he goes too far."

"Get the horses ready while I change!" She barked as she spun on her heel.

When she returned a few minutes later, she was warmly dressed and swung into the saddle of the only horse she ever rode, a large quarter horse gelding named Winchester. Although Ellen had definitely not invited him, Stephan also had mounted seeming a bit uncertain in the western saddle. Manuel mounted his smaller sturdy mustang after kissing an anxious looking Rosita on the cheek and led the group through the open gates into the valley. It was not hard to decipher the tracks of the four-wheeler over the patches of snow and thawing ground. Still, Char was leading the way ahead of the horses keeping his nose to the ground.

The tracks were following a very ancient trace along the rugged mountainside that they used for trail rides in the summer months. It narrowed in places so that it was barely the width of a standard four-wheeler along the rock face of the cliffs rising like an impenetrable wall. However, that perception of permanence was deceiving. At this time of year, the daytime thaws followed by nighttime freezing would loosen the rocks and boulders from the mountainside making rock falls and even landslides a more dangerous possibility. Ellen did not believe that the four-wheeler would be able to get very far in the rock-strewn trail. It was not long before they spotted it abandoned in the trail before a massive boulder that all but blocked the way even for the horses. As they edged around it, Char sniffed the still warm vehicle and then continued to forage ahead up the ever-climbing path.

The trail would continue precariously over the jagged mountain and along the top of the ridge before dropping to the other side. Even in the best of conditions, this was not an easy ride. Since the horses had spent the last five months snuggly in their stalls, they were not going to be able to continue at the pace they were going for very long. Winchester was breathing hard, and Ellen wondered if they should dismount and walk. Surely, they should catch up to Jack soon; it did not seem possible that he could have gotten that far in the hour that he had been missing. Time was also a factor, as they would have to gauge how far they had come and how long it would take them to return safely in the coming twilight hours. It was too dangerous to remain on the mountain overnight given the unpredictability of the wind and fire. The risk could increase astronomically in a matter of hours.

In front of them, Char lifted his head and caught the scent, then lowered it and moved furtively forward. He began loping faster now, and the horses quickened their pace. Then they heard and felt a horrendous rumbling like thunder, but it came from the mountain, not the sky. Char stopped quickly, head-up sharply and hurried back to Manuel. The horses also stopped, stamped, and whinnied restlessly at the vibration of the ground beneath their feet. Manuel turned back and said urgently but not loudly over his shoulder, "Rockslide! We must go carefully." He motioned to Char, who cautiously began again to move forward.

Five minutes later, rounding a bend, they could see the dust was still rising from the massive collapse of rocks that had tumbled off the mountain. Manuel raised his hand, and they reined their horses to a stop. Char was moving around the edges of the boulders and debris trying desperately to re-establish the scent. Abruptly, he halted and began to climb lightly over the rocks themselves. Panic clutched at her throat as Ellen looked from Char to the hillside above him. There was no way to gauge whether or not the remaining cliff above them was stable. Suddenly, the dog froze and peered through the rocks making digging motions with his front paws. Manuel leaped to the ground and began climbing carefully over the huge boulders to the place Char had indicated.

"My God!" thought Ellen "If one of those fell on him, he must be obliterated."

She and Stephan dismounted quickly. Stephan handed her the reins of his and Manuel's horses, motioning for her to stay with them. It was evident from his expression; he also thought there was little hope of finding Jack alive. When he reached Manuel, they began pulling at the rock debris with their hands. Unable just to stand there, Ellen hurriedly led the horses to the trees away from the hillside where she tied them, retrieving a saddle blanket, a water bottle, and some rope from Manuel's pack. Carefully, she began picking her way through the rubble of the fallen cliff side, so as not to dislodge any rocks that could trigger a further slide. The area where Stephan and Manuel were working appeared to be on the outer edge of the slide. When she reached them, Stephan said, "He's alive, but he's out cold, so we have no way to figure out how badly he is injured." She peered through the opening between two enormous boulders and could barely see the outline of his face.

"Is he trapped? Can we get him out?"

"We must clear these smaller pieces before we can tell" Manuel responded urgently but without feeling.

Ellen began lifting and removing the smaller rocks along where she thought his body should be. Soon she could feel his jeans and started moving along each leg lifting and clearing debris. Two huge boulders had fallen in such a way to block most of the large pieces from colliding with him. When they had cleared the area near his head, they found that he had a large gash on the side of his face that was bleeding profusely and had already begun to swell. Portions of his right hand reaching from under a large jagged rock appeared crushed, and when Manuel and Stephan lifted it, blood seeped from the smashed fingers. Quickly, Manuel made a make-shift tourniquet to slow the bleeding. It was apparent that while Jack might also have several more severe fractures, at the very least, he was going to be black and blue from the smaller rocks that had fallen on him.

Ellen left the blanket and water bottle with Manuel and returned to her saddle to radio Rosita about getting a rescue helicopter to their position. Finding them would not be a problem as they should be able to see the rock slide on the mountain from the air. Even as she spoke to Rosita, the whistling of the wind through the pines was ever increasing. While they were somewhat sheltered being on the inner rim of the valley, the helicopter would have brave the force of the wind to come across the mountains from the opposite ridge to reach them.

Her heart sank when Rosita responded that they were sending the helicopter, but the wind speed was elevating both the fire and the rescue danger. Ellen scrambled precariously back over the rock pile to relay the message. Manuel had managed to wrap a makeshift bandage with a scarf around Jack's head, and it appeared the bleeding was lessening. His hand was swelling and although not bleeding as extensively; it had a misshapen appearance that indicated several crushed bones. They managed to fashion a crude splint from the limited supplies they carried. He was now free enough from the rocks covering his body to make a more thorough investigation.

Other than the damage to his head and hand, it appeared that his torso had escaped major blows. In the process of examining him, Stephan had discovered the missing file zipped inside his jacket, as well as a deadly looking handgun. Having confiscated these, he gave them to Ellen to place in her saddlebags. Jack's breathing was shallow and ragged as he began to tremble with shock. They covered him as best they could with the spare saddle blanket. Ellen handed Manuel the water bottle to moisten Jack's lips. When the drops touched his lips, his eyelids fluttered slightly, and his body twitched.

"Manuel, do you think we should try to move him? What if another slide lets loose?" Ellen asked more anxious for the sake of Manuel and Stephan than she was for Jack.

"I think we will be ok, now that the sun has gone down behind the rim it will begin to freeze again and harden," Manuel assured her.

The sun had indeed gone behind the ridge, and the temperature was dropping rapidly. Ellen looked down at the figure lying at the base of the rubble as if he too had slid down the mountain. Did they dare move him? Stephan seemed to read her thoughts.

"Are you certain we shouldn't move him?" he inquired of Manuel.

"We do not know how badly he is injured. I think we should not try it unless it becomes necessary", he answered. Ellen mentally assessed their situation. The dropping temperatures chilled her, yet with the fire danger; it was too hazardous to consider even lighting a flare. They had warm jackets themselves but were not prepared to keep Jack warm enough. The ground on which he had fallen was at least somewhat thawed at the time of the slide. Now the creeping cold would begin to reach its icy fingers underneath Jack's battered body. The sun would not set for a couple more hours, but they were already in the darkening shadow of the mountain as it went down. If the rescue helicopter could not find them and successfully remove Jack soon, they would have to find their way down the precarious mountainside in total darkness.

Jack moved slightly and groaned. Manuel put a few more drops of water on his lips, and his eyes flicked open.

"Don't move," said Manuel gently, but firmly. "You were caught by a rock slide."

"You sir, are quite lucky to be alive," Stephan added in his clipped accent somewhat lacking in Manuel's warmth. Jack attempted to lift his right hand, winced, and paled.

"No target practice for a while I'm afraid," Stephan responded with significance. Jack's eyes flicked from one to the other, and he raised his left hand to his jacket tentatively. His eyes widened and flashed angrily.

"Well we couldn't exactly let the rescue helicopter pick you up with stolen documents and an illegal firearm, now could we?" Stephan spoke with dry sarcasm. Jack's angry grimace distorted his face.

"Not illegal! I have a license to carry! Let me up," he rasped, not liking his position of weakness. However, his attempt to sit upright, even with Manuel's supporting arm, caused him to gasp and his face to turn a sickly gray.

"Better lie still, there is no way to know how badly you are injured." Manuel encouraged resting him back on the ground. Jack began to shiver in spite of his coat, although there were beads of sweat on his pale gray face as shock and pain laid claim to his battered body. Manuel called Char to him and had him lay down somewhat reluctantly next to Jack's body for warmth.

"I'd better check on the helicopter," Ellen said turning away. Jack jerked his head in her direction as if he had not realized she was there also. His face distorted and his eyes squeezed shut as another stab of pain pierced his skull. Jack appeared about to lose consciousness when he motioned Stephan to lean closer.

"I wasn't stealing those documents," he wheezed forcing the words through his clenched teeth. "I had orders. I would have returned them. We needed some information." Stephan leaned forward anxious for Jack to answer before he lost consciousness.

"Is Martin still alive? Do you know where he is?" in his desperation, Stephan seemed ready to shake the injured man. As he slipped into oblivion, Jack managed to gasp in barely a whisper, "Matches description…don't know where… has information for us" his voice trailed off as he faded into painless oblivion.

Ellen had stopped moving and breathing as she strained to hear what Jack was saying and now caught her breath feeling as if the wind had been knocked out of her also. She moved forward automatically to get the radio and returning handed it to Manuel. Anxiety and despair gripped her by the throat so tightly she could not speak. Her thoughts were whirling, but not with hope. Someone who looked like Martin was somewhere no one could find with information for the authorities. It just could not be Martin. Beyond everything else, he had promised her that he would never work for any government.

The crackling of the radio static pulling Ellen back to reality. Rosita was relaying that the helicopter should be reaching them shortly when she abruptly switched to rapid animated Spanish. Ellen could see the muscles in Manuel's face tighten with anxiety. When he finished, she asked urgently, "What is it, Manuel?"

He was opening his mouth to answer when Char's head jerked upward, and he barked sharply. The sound of the search and rescue helicopter increased in intensity as it approached. They could only hope that the remaining mountainside was frozen enough to withstand the blast from the propellers or there would be another slide. They had no way to signal, but even in the deepening twilight, the sight of the rockslide was hard to miss. Soon a rescuer spiraled downward with an airlift stretcher dangling below him. Between them, the men were able to maneuver the stretcher to slide under Jack, who groaned and gasped. Before the rescue worker motioned to lift them back to the plane, he placed his mouth close to Manuel's ear and yelled something over the racket of the helicopter noise. Then he signaled and began slowly spiraling upward into the craft. When the helicopter had safely received its patient, it flew rapidly away.

"What's wrong?" Ellen said grasping Manuel's arm as he hurriedly gathered the supplies they had been using to help Jack.

"The fires!" he said with urgency moving as he packed. "The wind has turned them they are coming over the north ridge! He says he could see them coming rapido! He said keep going over the mountain."

Ellen was also instantly moving and mounting. There was no question of going over the mountain. She must get back to the Mission! An irrational anger seethed within her as if Jack himself was responsible for the menace bearing down upon them. First, he had destroyed her world of peace; now he brought the fires in his wake to finish it all. It was imperative that she evacuate the others; however, for a brief moment, she envisioned herself being consumed within the flaming walls of her refuge.

Quickly, this time, they moved down the perilous mountainside with Char going ahead and Manuel's mustang following him closely. The other horses had long been accustomed to following the sure-footed lead of the sturdy smaller horse and stayed close behind. The caustic smell of smoke blew into their faces with the wind. Even though it was not thick enough to be dangerous, Ellen covered her face with a scarf as if to defend herself from the offending fumes. It was getting darker, and as they descended, they caught sight through the trees of the advancing trail of light along the top of the ridge ahead of them at the end of the valley. The flashes of fire looked so harmless; as though the mountains were covered in the ancient campfires of the tribes gathering for a powwow. However, the bitter reality was, at the rate that it was moving and with the wind strongly in their direction; it could be upon them in just a matter of hours.

The sight spurred them forward at a precarious pace. By the time, the three of them swung from their mounts in the courtyard the animals were lathered with sweat from their exertions. Rosita was waiting, quickly helping to unsaddle, but instead of stabling the horses, she loaded them into the waiting horse trailer. All the time she spoke rapid and urgent Spanish to Manuel. The police had come to tell them to evacuate, and she had sent Heather, James, and Mr. Johnson with them. The police would transport the guests to a friend's dude ranch/bed and breakfast down in the valley near Alamogordo where Stephan and Rosita would join them bringing the horses. Rosita could show the way, and Stephan assured them he had driven many a "horse box" growing up in the English countryside. Vaguely, Ellen realized that this was not the usual treatment for a paying guest, but there was nothing else to do. Char should go also, but if he were gone, she would have no reason to make an effort to survive. Hopelessness enveloped her like the gathering smoke, choking out her will to live; everyone she loved seemed so far away or lost.

Manuel held his wife close to him for a moment whispering then they crossed themselves and kissed gently; even their parting was a prayer. On the last occasion when a fire evacuation order had come, Ellen had tried to force Manuel to leave. He had smiled sadly nodding toward the church.

"But what about the Señoras? They will come." They had come, the small bent figures with their starched black dresses and white prayer shawls, shuffling softly

to the altar to kneel and make their supplications for deliverance. Ellen had wondered at the time where their families were and why they did not stop them from
coming. This time, Ellen did not attempt a protest. Manuel quickly began to prepare for the siege by fire, repeating the practices that had occurred so often in his
many years at the Mission as to seem almost automatic. As Ellen was quickly gathering her most valuable items into a leather satchel along with the folder Jack had
taken, her anger returned, but this time as a friend. She could not just give up and
wait for the fires to consume her; she would never know the truth! Why suddenly
after two years did these men think Martin was alive? There had to be a reason,
and the reason must be a compelling one for Stephan to come from overseas to
find her, even for Jack to be willing to take the risks that he had taken. She was
not about to lay down and die without knowing what that was! Maybe the answer
was still here. Her only fear now was that the fires would reach her before she
discovered the truth; she strode with determination across the courtyard to the
guest rooms.

Chapter 4

Jack's room was first, and with total disregard for her guest's privacy or rights, Ellen began dismantling his suitcase. It was to no avail, whatever information he had about Martin was not in the room; although she made a thorough examination of every possible hiding place. In fact, other than clothing, there was nothing left in the room that would have in any way identified the inhabitant. She found no traces, even with the help of Char prowling around the room searching with her. Finally, Ellen left, not even bothering to lock the door behind her.

The next room was Stephan's and this time Ellen's conscience did prick causing her to hesitate for a moment. Even though he scarcely seemed like a guest now, if the Mission escaped the flames, Stephan would surely be back. It would not do for him to return to a ransacked room. Ellen brushed the thought aside as she turned the lock; somehow, it did not matter to her anymore.

His room was neat and tidy, every bit the British gentleman. The only thing Ellen found of interest was a worn leather bag with a locked flap cover. Surely, he would have taken it with him if he had been given the time to return to his room. Rosita had taken his suitcase for him but had not considered this case essential. There was no key to be found to unlock it, but if it was upended, Ellen found that she could slip papers from the gap under the flap lid. However, it was not a paper that she first extracted, but a thin plastic pouch full of pictures.

The pictures were of Martin and various men including Stephan, some of whom she recognized, some she did not. Then there were pictures of herself and her children at Martin's memorial service. Had Stephan been there? She certainly did not remember ever meeting him, but that did not mean he had not been there. Ellen looked at the blank, empty, hollow-eyed face in the photo that was her own. It was all a blur to her even now. A nightmarish haze.

There were pictures of her children from the memorial service also; their faces were as sad and empty as her own. She sighed heavily, a sob catching in her throat. Her children. It seemed that what they were missing the most now was not their father; instead, it was the possibility of ever knowing him. He had always seemed distracted from them by greater, higher things. Ellen had never doubted that he loved them and wanted the best for them. He had held great aspirations and goals for them. However, the eldest became a writer, not a minister. The second became an artist, not a teacher. The third became an aid worker and human rights activist, not the missionary his father wanted. The youngest had gone to study in Canada, choosing to become a biologist studying tundra species rather than the pastor of his grandfather's little country church.

Somehow, Martin had never understood that his wise advice, even his discipline, needed more than logic and even righteousness as a foundation; it needed a relationship. Maybe, if he could have included them in his work, they would have caught his vision of the significance and importance of it. But they were all excluded because it wasn't safe, or the children had school, or there was never enough money in the budget for the extra ticket. Instead, even as they tried to understand, they resented the calling that took him away and excluded them. She had done the best she could, but somehow, they would always long for the relationship they had never had.

When she turned the leather bag again with an impatient shake, a black and white photo paper-clipped to a card and wrapped in tissue paper slipped from the bag. Ellen held it closely under the bedside lamp. It appeared to have been taken from the front of a vehicle toward the back seat where a man in a blindfold was wedged between two bearded men with guns. Panic followed by nausea nearly overwhelmed her. Was it Martin? Ellen sank onto the bedside. Grasping the photo tightly to steady her trembling hands, she studied it intently. He had a beard like Martin's, silvery white. His hands were in front of him, but she could not tell if they were restrained. The reality of the photo seemed to crystallize all her worst fears and premonitions.

So, this was it! Jack and Stephan wanted to know if this blindfolded man was Martin. Even if it was he, it still probably meant that by now he was not alive. Trying to steady her shaking frame, Ellen grasped the picture forcefully with both hands, her knuckles turning white. Willing herself to focus in spite of the waves of fear and dread threatening to devastate her, she still could see only vaguely the lower half of his face and body. His clothes were western with dark colored pants and what looked like a black jacket. There was nothing to distinguish it as Martin's clothing although he often wore dark colors. She could not determine whether he was wearing a watch or a wedding ring.

Still clutching the photo, Ellen screamed when the room suddenly went black. Staggering to her feet swaying from shock and disoriented, after nearly tripping over Char, she grasped his collar letting him lead her to the door. Slipping the photo into her inner jacket pocket, she stumbled toward the flickering light near the door of the chapel. Manuel was standing there waving a flashlight and looked relieved to see her.

"I think the fire has taken out the transformer!" he gestured urgently toward the glowing, snaking flames whipping through the trees ever closer. He guided Ellen into the candle-lit interior of the chapel.

"I opened the spring gates," he said reassuringly. The spring gates were a series of channels leading from the spring, the acequia madre, that had once been used to irrigate the fields where the Padres had grown their maize, chilies, and other crops. Manuel had maintained the channels closer to the Mission with the intention of flooding what had once been fields and creating water breaks. Wind-driven fires could quickly jump the ditches, but the brush and trees had also been cleared some distance from the adobe walls for added fire prevention.

"There may not be time for them to flood," Manuel looked with concern at Ellen's face in the candlelight.

She was pale and trembling still clutching Char's collar. It did not even appear that she was listening. He guided her into a pew and returned quickly to place a glass of water into her trembling hands. Gently, he raised the glass in her hands helping her, as one would assist a child. Ellen felt divided from herself. As if while her body was sitting below her in the candlelit church, her spirit looked on, reluctant to stay with her in her trauma.

At that moment, the door of the chapel creaked open, and the procession began. Five elderly bent figures shuffled past them in ghostly procession as if they were rustling shadows. They moved sedately to the altar rail and knelt with clasp hands and faces raised to the crucifix. Ellen did not even realize that she had followed them until a soft bony hand gently took hers, urging her to kneel with them.

Slowly, the aged voices began their prayers, and Ellen felt surrounded by their petitions as in a cloud. She could not raise her head, but gradually she felt the peace of their faith permeate her spirit. This was the end then; surely, she would die here. Like this. Bowing in submission to God, she would cease struggling. What did she have to fight for, or live for now? Martin had almost certainly died at the hands of those men. Inevitably, the Mission would soon be consumed. This sanctuary would be her sepulcher. She would let it all go. She would let herself go. The soul, which now found the body too painful to inhabit, she would release. Would it go to God?

"Father, have mercy on me a sinner, not my will, but yours be done. Into your hands, I commit my spirit." She groaned with her head heavy against the altar rail.

She did not realize she had slipped fainting to the floor until she felt the wet lick of Char on her hand. Gradually, warmth entered her body giving her strength to open her eyes. She could see it then in the flickering light, the crucifix, the dying Christ. With an expression of painful acceptance on the face, the light slanted off the smooth marble as if tears moistened his eyes. Sudden comprehension dawned with her returning consciousness, and she realized; he knew!

He had experienced loss; he even knew the agony that Martin had likely endured at the hands of those men because he also had suffered at the hands of sinful men. He had felt the abandonment of being forsaken by all, even the Father. For the first time since Martin had disappeared, she did not feel forsaken; because He knew. Freely, her tears were flowing as she struggled to raise herself, only then realizing that Manuel was gently supporting her head with tears on his face, as well. Around them, the elderly women knelt with clasped hands and raised faces while Char whined softly.

Ellen wrenched herself to her knees, crawling to grasp the altar rail, she rested her throbbing head upon it. "Here Father, I lay down my life, my sacrifice, my all! Consume me! Consume it all if you will!" She gasped raggedly.

Ellen could not tell if what she felt was peace or numbness. The struggle and rage had left her. Maybe she was just empty. Shakily grasping Manuel's arm, she rose to her feet and gently embraced the small bent figures with their faces of tender concern. Char pressed to her side as she unsteadily grasped the ends of the pews and made her way thru the wavering light of the candlelit church. Manuel would have accompanied her, but she gestured for him to remain with the circle of bent figures. He pressed his flashlight into her clammy hands as she stepped into the arched corridor.

The choking smell of burning startled her and brought some sense of reality back to her shocked system. Ellen wrapped her scarf around her nose and mouth as she walked haltingly toward the front entrance with one hand supporting herself against the inner wall of the corridor. It seemed to take all her strength to shove the heavy doors open toward the valley. The fires cut jagged gashes of angry red across the face of the hills on the north side of the valley walls. The wind thrashed the flames closer to the ridgeline into raging, rapidly moving torrents of inferno. Lower, further down the hills, the fires moved more slowly due to the decrease in the winds and the damper snow-melted ground. Still, it moved inexorably forward. Carefully, with one hand against the thick outside wall of the Mission, Ellen began edging her way around the Mission in the direction of the fire. The fire now ran along the brink of the ridge very near where they had been earlier at the landslide. Vaguely, Ellen realized that the stolen four-wheeler would be incinerated. Jack's theft and threat seemed irrelevant to her now, although only a few hours had passed.

The deadly fingers of flame were closest to the chapel corner of the Mission. Then, as Ellen looked toward the base of the hill, to her alarm there appeared to be molten fire, as if the mountain had been torn to its core and was draining its liquid substance on the valley floor. Her disoriented panic became relief when her next step splashed into water covering her ankle. What she saw was not fire, but the reflection of the blaze on the flooded ground! For the moment, Manuel's plan seemed to be working. There was only hope if the wind did not increase sufficiently to create a firestorm which would leap the ditches in its voracious search for fuel.

Ellen continued feeling her way along the thick outside wall to the entrance until she grasped the heavy metal latch of the chapel doors. Only after slipping into the candle-lit sanctuary did Ellen realize how intense the smoke had become outside its thick walls. She was coughing, and Char sneezed as she handed the flashlight to Manuel reporting to him what she had seen. As he slipped into the darkness, Ellen stretched out on a wooden pew overwhelmed with exhaustion. She did not intend to sleep, and so awoke disoriented to beams of light penetrating the murky dimness from the opened chapel door. The thick hazy dawn was pierced by the flashing lights of ambulances and the fire engines of a very weary looking fire-fighting crew.

Somehow, just seeing their soot smeared, smoke-darkened faces mobilized her to action. Ignoring their pleas for her evacuation, she set about assembling what meals she could manage with no electricity. Everything refrigerated would need to be disposed of if it was not eaten quickly anyway. Even the rooms so recently occupied by guests became emergency resting places for crews needing a break from the exhaustion of many hours battling the expanding blaze. Soon the Mission became a hive of activity, which only increased as evening fell. Ellen felt strangely relieved to be overwhelmed. She did not need to think, just work. The gratitude she saw in the faces of the hungry and haggard firefighters soothed her soul. Maybe God did not need Wayfaring Mission to be consumed to accept her offering. Maybe it could become a mission again, and her life could find some meaning through this crisis.

The blazing inferno continued to spread rapidly along the ridges before extending its scorching grasp toward the valley floor. Throughout the day, planes dropped water and chemicals from the air on the upper ridges while crews worked from below to keep the fire from creeping down the mountain. The real danger would intensify if the flames made it around the valley to the opposite side of the Mission where the road lay. It led to a small resort village, and that highway was the only firebreak that existed on the southern end of the Mission. Here there were no fields to flood; only the road that ran against the mountainside. The fire had to be conquered in this valley before it crossed the peaks and endangered the homes and businesses in the mountain community.

As evening approached, the battle increased as reinforcement crews arrived determined to prevent the fire from passing over the mountain or the road. Several firefighters had to be returned to the Mission carried by emergency crews requiring the dining room to become a recovery and triage center for the injured. Ellen was careful to avoid the news team that somehow had managed to accompany the advancing fire crews and emergency personnel. Reports from the fire crews indicated that unless the wind changed or dropped in intensity on the ridges, there would be no way to stem the advancing flames. Ellen slipped from the crowded triage room and made her way to the chapel with several water bottles for the Señoras. Still, the fragile hunched figures took their turns holding vigil at the altar rail. After delivering them, Ellen slid into a darkened pew, and Char dropped exhausted to the floor at her feet.

A shaft of light pierced the dim interior as the door open and closed softly. Ellen leaned further back into the shadow as a figure walked past her. Stephan moved into a bench toward the front and dropped to his knees bowing his head. From the darkness, Ellen studied him, feeling the picture still in her coat pocket like a dead weight on her heart. With the sharpness dulled, only the heaviness remained. The chronic ache of loss, so familiar had returned. As if sensing her presence or her eyes on him, Stephan turned and looked into her eyes in the dim shadows. Ellen saw him shudder slightly at the sight of her haggard face. The loss of sleep and grueling activities shown in the dark shadows of her eyes and her unkempt hair. Silently, she held his eyes unable to veil the loss that lived there. Stephan looked away brushing his hand over his eyes. Quietly he rose and came to join her.

"Your bag is in my office," she related flatly. "We needed the room for the crews to rest."

"Of course," he responded nodding.

"Except for this," Ellen said pulling out the photo from her pocket wincing as her eyes were drawn to the blindfolded figure. Without looking at him, she stood placing the picture back into her pocket and turning left the chapel. Ellen did not realize he had followed her until she unlocked her office and found him behind her. She reached inside and handed him his satchel.

"If you are staying, you can set up a cot in the great room." She gestured toward the dining room. "The rescue personnel have a few cots left, I think. I could use some help in the kitchen."

"Why don't you rest for a bit?" Stephan pleaded with genuine concern.

Ellen stared at him blankly as if sleep were a foreign concept. Instead of answering, she relocked her door and led the way through the evening haze and gloom toward the kitchen. The rescue crews had brought generators, and Manuel had found some old kerosene lanterns that gave sufficient light for them to begin assembling nearly everything remaining in the pantry into sandwiches, fruit, and vegetable platters. Stephan made a couple half-hearted attempts at conversation, but Ellen seemed to be an automaton moving without emotion or words. They delivered the trays to the tables where the rescue workers passing through could pause for some refreshments. Stephan spoke quietly to one of the EMTs who was walking by on his way to the makeshift triage room in the dining room.

When a firm hand grasped her elbow, Ellen looked into the face of a frowning nurse who resolutely guided her down the corridor to her office in spite of her protests. Patiently, the nurse waited for her to unlock her door and carefully guided her up the stairs to her bed. Ellen only took the time to remove her jacket and boots before falling across her bed. Char collapsed on the rug beside her. She held the photo in her hand as she drifted off into an exhausted sleep. Her dreams were as dark and smoky as the night. Shadowy figures of men thrust Martin into the vehicle. They were dark, vaporous silhouettes with threatening accents and angry shouts. He looked at her but did not speak, although Ellen screamed his name; he did not seem to hear. They were leaving! She was screaming, trying to run after them, but her feet were tangled in the long robe she was wearing. Then the dream's colors were running down, washing away like watercolors splashed on canvas. Maybe it was fading with her tears.

Char's growling pulled Ellen abruptly from the grasp of the nightmare. Quickly, wiping the tears from her eyes, she snapped on the flashlight she had laid beside her bed. Char was standing bolt upright facing the stairs to her room. The hackles on his neck stood up fiercely. When Ellen tried to stand, she realized the robe from her dream was probably the covers of her bed now wound around her feet. Managing to untangle herself, she released Char with a word who bounded down the stairs growling fiercely. There followed a rapid thudding and a quickly slammed door. Who had been there? It could not have been Jack; there was no way he could move so rapidly in his battered state; he was probably still in the hospital.

In a panic, Ellen groped around on the bed frantically until she found the photo. Tucking it into her shirt pocket and slipping back into her jacket against the chill, she edged carefully down the stairs. Flashing the light around her office, she saw a couple of drawers opened, but apparently, the intruder had just begun his search when Char had alerted her. He must have been as worn out as she was not to have heard the intruder sooner. To her chagrin, Ellen realized that in her exhaustion she had not locked either her office or her apartment door when the nurse had left after taking her upstairs to her room.

Opening the door to the courtyard Ellen smelled a smoky dampness like the odor of an extinguished campfire. A cloudy mist was falling through the early dawn light. Relief flooded over her as she realized the danger at least for Wayfaring Mission was passed. Ellen hurried to find Manuel in the chapel. He was gently assisting the little women into a sleek black antique car that had mysteriously arrived at the perfect time. Ellen held their frail hands, thanking them tenderly in her broken Spanish for their prayers and kindness in her hour of travail. How ghostly their figures appeared in the vaporous half-light, rather like ephemeral saints or even angels. As their taillights disappeared into the soot-stained mist, they passed the headlights of two other vehicles approaching. One was the truck and trailer that Rosita had taken to transport the horses. Behind it, she saw another four-wheel drive vehicle. Rosita stepped from the truck and into Manuel's waiting arms. Ellen watched their relief and affection through her tears with a painful lump in her throat.

Chapter 5

Ellen ignored the other vehicle, assuming it was either more media or part of the rescue teams until she heard someone call, "Mom!" Instinctively, she whirled toward the sound she knew could only be the voice of her eldest son! They were all there, all four of her children climbing out of the rental jeep. Clutching them to her, she was overwhelmed with relief. She understood the sacrifice they would have made to rearrange their schedules, to coordinate a meeting in Albuquerque, and then to drive the four plus hours to get to the Mission. Holding each one seemed to be gathering fragmented parts of herself into wholeness. Until this moment, she had not even realized how much she needed them close to her. Of course, they did not understand the depth of her feelings; they could only assume it was a reaction to her fears for herself and the Mission.

"We saw the Mission in the news coverage of the fire. We thought you might need some help, either picking up the pieces or moving on," her daughter reassured holding Ellen in a tight embrace.

"But what about your jobs, school, families?" She asked tearfully, looking into each precious face.

"No problem Mom. We've got all that taken care of," Said her oldest dismissively. "Now where do we start?"

Immediately, they began working, helping the various crews that were packing to proceed to the next phase of the crisis, and assisting Rosita, who had returned with abundant supplies, restore order to her kitchen. While there was no electricity to wash linens, once the crews left with their generators, they were still able to change the beds and to clean the guest rooms as much as possible. Ellen sighed with relief as she watched them. If nothing else, somehow her children had all learned the value of hard work. Throughout the day, the crews left one by one, each full of gratitude for the assistance the Mission had provided them. Finally, when Rosita called them to sit down to dinner only Manuel, Ellen, her four children, and Stephan were left. In the candlelight, Manuel raised his hands and prayed; thanking God for deliverance once again with the confidence of one who had never doubted his gracious God.

When Ellen opened her eyes after wiping her tears, she could see the questions on the faces of her sons as they looked toward Stephan. Who was this man who had worked so hard with them all day? They had first assumed he was with one of the crews, but when they were all gone; Stephen remained. What was his relationship with her? What was he doing there?

Reluctantly, Ellen gestured from Stephan to each of her children introducing them; although judging from the pictures she had found in his room, she assumed he was already well aware of their names.

"Stephan knew your father and supported him in his ministry." She explained without feeling. She watched the parade of emotions that crossed their faces. Their expressions indicated that the introduction still did not clarify his presence there. For now, she chose to postpone the explanations. Ellen could not help smiling when she noticed her eldest, the only fluent Spanish speaker questioning Manuel in a quiet voice. For the rest of them, their conversation was about the fire, the heroic firefighters, the emergency medical teams, and the Senoras. The chilling mist that had mercifully settled over the area had provided just enough moisture for the crews finally to contain the raging blaze, even though it was within sight of the small mountain village.

With their usual cheerful camaraderie, they all helped Rosita to clean up after dinner by the light of the lanterns and were rewarded with steaming mugs of her chocolate, heated in a larger pot hung over the open flames, as they sat around the fire with candlelight flickering around the great room. It was time, she must tell them about the photo, but Ellen felt paralyzed with the awareness of the renewed sense of loss it would bring. Somewhat hoarsely, she asked Manuel to bring his high-powered flashlight. Taking it from him with shaking hands, and holding the picture under the light in front of her, she spoke miserably, "This is why Stephan is here. He came to ask me about this."

Ellen was not certain that this was true; he might never have shown it to her at all. Still, Stephan remained sitting in the background, silent in the shadows. They each, in turn, examined the photo as meticulously as was possible with the light they had. Their faces went pale one after another in a wave of progressive shock.

Her daughter came to her side as tears began to flow. Confusion and anxiety overwhelmed them as they struggled to comprehend what they were seeing; gradually the questions started.

"So, when did this happen? I don't understand; Dad was captured sometime before the plane crash?" one asked.

"We believe he was probably not on the airplane when it went down," Stephan answered gently as if his tone could somehow lessen the blow his words would give. This time, his words only momentarily stunned them into silence.

"What, so you mean he wasn't on the plane? He was on the passenger list!" another questioned.

"That airline does not have a good safety record or security protocol. There is a real possibility that they never checked the passenger's identification; just produced the list after the flight went down." Stephan explained.

"Are you certain that this is him?" someone challenged.

"No, but the photo was retrieved from the area where we believe he may have been traveling," said Stephan seriously.

"Do you have any idea who these men are? What group they are with?" they wanted to know.

"No, but their appearance suggests some possibilities," Stephan answered vaguely. The questions began to get more demanding and angry as the first wave of shock began to subside.

"How long have you known about this?" the eldest wanted to know.

"For about six months, but I only received the photo a month ago," Stephan added quickly. It was approximately six months ago when he had booked his reservation at the Mission, Ellen thought absently.

"Has anyone done anything about this? Contacted the authorities! Attempted to find him?" the eldest demanded.

"If the motive for his kidnapping were ransom, or to make a statement, we would have expected whoever was holding him to have contacted us two years ago. There was never a message." Stephan risked a glance at Ellen and continued, "The US authorities would like to find him because they think these men belong to a group near where they are currently fighting. They believe that if he is still alive, he could give them valuable information on their enemies."

At their bewildered looks of incredulity, Ellen briefly and matter-of-factly, described their encounters with Jack. Everyone sat perfectly still, as the full import of what was said fell on their shocked and saddened consciousness. It suddenly dawned on Ellen that they all seemed convinced that it was their father in the photo!

"Why do you think it is him?" She asked earnestly, as she searched their faces. They all looked away, each one struggling with his or her private pain.

"It just feels like him," said her daughter Kate, who had always been the most intuitive, with a perception that sometimes bordered on foresight.

"And he always wore black," she added sadly ruefully shrugging her shoulders.

"He doesn't look afraid. His body in the photo doesn't appear tense," muttered Richard the youngest, who in spite of his move to Canada hated to travel and had always been in awe of his father's intrepid nature. Ellen turned to her two skeptics, Andrew the oldest most guarded one, and Chris the second son who was rash and impetuous.

"It doesn't matter if it's him, does it? If there is even a possibility that he is still alive, we have to investigate!" Chris snapped angrily.

"I agree, we have no choice but to follow whatever leads are available," said Andrew firmly with resolution.

"There is another interpretation that I must mention," Stephan cleared his throat speaking reluctantly, "What if he was not taken a prisoner in that photograph? He may have gone there by invitation, but had to be blindfolded as a precaution. They might have wanted to ensure that he could not reveal their location if he were ever taken into custody by Jack or his friends." There was a moment of astonished silence.

"Why do you think that? Did you send him there?" Chris spoke with angry accusation.

Stephan bent his head slightly as if the words were a blow.

"He went where he felt he should go. We may have paid the way, but we did not dictate which 'invitations' he should accept." He spoke sadly with regret.

"He said he felt they needed to be told that there was another prophet, Isa, who taught of love, not jihad."

Ellen strode angrily across the room to blaze the flashlight full in his face,

"So, you did know! You knew where he was going? What was the point of coming here to question me about his location if you already knew?" This time, her voice held the accusation.

"That was all the information we had! Just that statement. He didn't tell us when, or even where he would be going! He was just letting us know that he would not turn down an opportunity if it came." His voice pleaded for understanding as he glanced around at the angry indictment in the faces looming into the circle of light.

The reality was that he had completely disregarded them in his dealings with Martin. Somehow, the fact that Martin had kept this part of his life, his family, so separate from his work had allowed Stephan to consider them as irrelevant to it. Ellen dropped back into a chair with her head in her hands. Kate came and sat beside her with tears in her eyes. Ellen had been trying to process this information for days. If she was still reeling, what must it be like for them?

Unexpectedly, Char got up quickly from where he was sitting alert to the tension in the room and moved toward the door. Manuel followed him and opened it to James and Heather. They looked somewhat anxious peering in through the dim candlelight, which triggered Ellen's automatic reactions as an innkeeper. Quickly, she introduced them to her children, arranged for their luggage, thanked her friends from the ranch for providing for them, and then settled them into the soft leather chairs with chocolate in their hands. They sat closely together holding hands. Apparently, in spite of their holiday disruptions, being refugees from the fire had not harmed their growing relationship; it appeared to be thriving. They seemed determined to finish out their stay, more for the opportunity to be together than for the adventure it had become.

"But where is Mr. Johnson? Did he not stay at the ranch?" Ellen asked abruptly.

James smiled slightly, "he chose to stay at the casino, so I have no idea when he will return. That could depend on how much money he has left."

"Oh dear, well I guess he could claim he had no other choice, there aren't many hotels in this area. Although, I am not confident that his wife will buy that story."

She added wryly. She would need to see about transporting his designer luggage; since apparently, he was not going to finish out his stay at the Mission.

With Ellen's help, Manuel arranged for everyone's sleeping quarters, checked on their supplies, and made a list of necessary provisions. She also watched her children responding to the young people. Kate, the artist, had instantly spotted the ever-present sketchbook under Heather's arm and before long was examining it closely by the candlelight. Andrew and James had discovered some mutual contacts within the entertainment industry and were sharing stories. As was his nature, her gentle giant, Richard was standing beside Manuel, waiting to carry and help with whatever task was at hand. However, Chris was not in the room, and neither was Stephan.

Finishing her supply assessment quickly, she left Manuel and Richard to carry bedding, luggage, candles, and flashlights to the guest rooms. She discovered Chris and Stephan in the library huddled over a map spread out on the table; peering intently by the light of their flashlights. Ellen's heart warmed a bit. With this son, there was always a map involved no matter what crisis or adventure was afoot. He had his father's wanderlust and frequently volunteered for assignments with various aid projects that took him to the most remote locations. She could hear the intensity of his voice.

"I can get into these areas because my organization is already there providing aid, vaccinations, and education resources, but we are also unpopular for those very same reasons since we have not limited education only to boys. Also in some of these areas, you can be shot for trying to vaccinate children or for giving polio drops. I think if I went in here unless I stumbled on him accidentally, no one would voluntarily give me information. They would be too afraid of retaliation." Chris pointed out locations on the map as he spoke.

Ellen could not help feeling her heart tightening within her. This child had always alarmed her with his desire for life on the edge. There was not much caution in his nature. His younger brother used to say about him that Chris was missing the little voice in his head that should be telling him what he was about to do was not a good idea. Did it matter that she could not bear the thought of another of the men in her life disappearing into the void? It was true that he was the only one with the contacts and platform to enter the country. He was also the one most likely to go where angels feared to tread.

Stephan was the first to realize her presence in the room. When he turned, and looked at her gaunt face in the flickering candlelight, with a guilty expression, he quickly rolled up the map. Chris looked around with annoyance. When he saw her in the dim light, the defiance that had always been part of his nature rose to the surface. Oblivious to her feelings, he began his argument, "Mother, you know I am the only one who can get even close to where he is supposed to be! I will have access to translators, and the protection of an international aid organization! It is still a long shot, but at least, we should attempt. We cannot just leave him out there! It is so dangerous and, well, he's not as young as he used to be…" His voice had gone from challenging to pleading.

Ellen had dropped into a chair with her head in her hands. She felt a hand on each of her shoulders, Kate on one side and Richard on the other. They had come when they heard the upraised voices. She saw through her tears Andrew face-off before Chris and heard the hard edge in his voice.

"Her concern is not about Dad, Chris! Chances are, they murdered him two years ago. She doesn't want to lose you too! You have to face the facts that even if you were not in danger, it would be a miracle if you found him alive!" He spoke the reality harshly. The authority he had always somehow been intrinsically given in the lives of his siblings by his seniority, still seemed to be in effect. Chris dropped his chin and looked away.

Andrew turned to Stephan asking sharply, "Have you had that photo analyzed? Have you taken it to anyone who could tell what sort of camera, photo paper, age or anything?"

Stephan shook his head sadly.

"We were too afraid to let the authorities get knowledge of its existence. If they already know, then that may be why Jack was here, at least in part."

Kate stepped forward eagerly, "I know someone who can do it! Dirk Watson. He's a forensic photographer who taught some of my undergrad photography classes. Besides, he owes me a favor; I haven't revealed that he keeps certain mushrooms for personal use. He is currently doing an exhibition up in Taos this month, not of his forensic work, of course, so he is even in the state! He is the last person who would turn something over to the feds!"

Kate's brothers grinned at her rambling description, and Ellen was grateful for the break in the tension; although she could see the disfavor on Stephan's face. Trusting their only clue to this artsy addict person did not seem wise to him. However, over the years, Ellen had learned to trust her daughter in her choice of offbeat friends. They were always somewhat bizarre, but they were also loyal with hearts of gold. The positive attributes that only Kate could see in them, she also somehow managed to draw out of them. Even Josiah, the mountain man from Montana that Kate had married, though he seemed rough around the edges, had turned out to be patient, kind, and loving. Smiling at Stephan's discomfort, she retrieved an envelope from her desk, slipped the photo into it, handing it to Kate.

"Just don't lose it between here and there!" she ordered. Richard chuckled, and Kate glared at him. Her absent-mindedness and attention deficit tendencies were legendary with her siblings.

"Wait a minute, that's it?" Chris demanded harshly, "When every moment counts, we are going to sit on our hands waiting for some pot-smoking geek to leave the haze long enough to analyze it!" Kate gave him an aggrieved look, which he ignored.

"It is not that we don't think you should go, Chris!" Andrew shot back glancing at Ellen as he spoke, "You just need to think before you act, take some sensible precautions, and lower your expectations."

"I could go with him," Stephan's voice sounded distant from outside the circle of the candlelight.

"I feel quite responsible for what happened to all of you." He spoke sadly and stepping forward into the lighted circle caught Ellen's eye.

"I do still have some home office contacts. Do you think there is there any way your organization will let me go with you on a somewhat unofficial fact-finding tour of the region?" he directed the question to Chris.

Chris stepped forward eagerly, "I am sure I can find a way!"

Stephan came to stand with military erectness before Ellen. Drawing himself up as a soldier to attention, he spoke gravely with humble dignity, "Ellen, I realize that I, and his other supporters, bear some responsibility for the loss of Martin. I commit to you that I will protect, and return your son safely to you or die in the attempt to do so! Please allow us to proceed with the arrangements as soon as possible; time is of the essence."

Ellen saw the smirk pass behind Stephan's back between her children. She nodded sadly and solemnly to Stephan's sincerity. Even as they mocked his proper British gentleman bravado; they all recognized, first of all, that no one could stop Chris, and second that Stephan had no idea what he was undertaking. Sighing, Ellen looked at the clock feeling suddenly so weary. Absently, she wondered if Manuel had taken care of James and Heather, but somehow, she was certain that he had. Dragging herself to her feet, she hugged each of her children good night and called Char who had been leaning against the silent Richard while he stroked him gently letting the conversation whirl around them.

As her foot hit the last step of the staircase to her room, the ceiling lights flickered, then began to glow brightly. A spontaneous cheer burst from the group below her in the library bringing an involuntary smile to her lips. Her sentiments exactly, thank goodness for electricity! Her children would be up until the wee hours discussing, planning, and debating. It was always their custom when they could be together, even when there was not something as momentous as this situation hanging over them. The fact that they all enjoyed spending time with each other was a blessing she would never take for granted; rather like the benefits of electricity.

Ellen glanced around at her now lighted room realizing that the chaos her life had become in just four short days seemed reflected in the disarray around her. As she mechanically began tidying her room, she tried to remember when she could even have made such a mess. Char paced restlessly around the room, on alert and sniffing. He had stopped over what appeared to be a scrap of paper.

It was a playing card, the ace of hearts. Not being a card player herself, she could not imagine how it could have ended up in her room. Was there even a single deck of cards in the whole mission? She certainly did not remember ever purchasing any. The only one interested in cards was surely Mr. Johnson, and he had been gone for two days. Maybe she had somehow gotten it attached to her clothing when she was cleaning out his room for the firefighters, but she did not remember seeing any decks of cards there either. So here was yet another unanswered question. Ellen sighed; she was just too tired.

Throughout the night, Ellen was occasionally roused by bursts of laughter or loud exclamations from the group gathered in the rooms below her. However, this time, she did not feel alarmed but comforted. The presence of her loved ones, even in the midst of her current anxiety, brought a relief that she could only describe as wholeness. Even Char was able to stretch out by the balcony door and though his ears twitched at the outbursts, he never once began the pacing which had become his nightly routine. They had the first truly restful sleep that Ellen could remember for days.

Chapter 6

In spite of her fatigue, Ellen woke, as early as usual, the next morning. If only it were possible for her to sleep late, but it was not likely for her once the sun was shining. Incredibly, her sleep had been free of dark and troubling dreams. The presence of her children and the fact that she was no longer carrying the full weight of Martin's disappearance or death alone, gave her, if not hope, at least strength to face whatever was ahead. After a luxuriously long and blessedly hot shower, she dressed, sticking the playing card in her pocket, and went quickly downstairs. With Char at her heels, she found Rosita in the kitchen humming and cooking. Ellen smiled and hugged her shoulder gently as she cooked. Then she set about giving Char an extra portion of food for all his attentive care the past few days. It was such a blessing to have such beautiful souls to share one's life. Rosita waved her spatula at her smiling, "Ah, Mamá is so happy with her children here!"

"Si! I never know how much I miss them until I see them again." Ellen confessed wistfully; as she took the tray that Rosita had filled to the dining area to set up the breakfast buffet. She was so busy with her work that she did not notice Stephan enter until she heard an enormous yawn behind her. Ellen jumped slightly but smiled when she saw him.

"What time did they finally go to bed last night?" She grinned somewhat mischievously.

"I am not certain since I abandoned them around two o'clock, but they seemed to be going strong still." He answered stifling another yawn.

"You do realize you are proposing to accompany the worst sleep offender I have ever met to the other side of the world? I never successfully managed to teach Chris how to go to bed on time. He has always come alive after eleven pm." She warned lightheartedly.

"I guess I may have to resort to the use of stimulants!" He answered grasping the coffee pot instead of his usual tea.

After he had sat down with his coffee, and toast, Ellen took a seat across from him and laid the playing card between them. Stephan studied it with a raised eyebrow, "Got any more aces up your sleeve? We could sure use some!" his chuckle died when he looked at her face.

"I found that when I was straightening my room last night. And I don't play cards, do you?" she asked with a slight tone of accusation.

"No, I do not," he said hesitating as he turned the card over in his hand. The center of the back of the card held geometric shapes, and there were designs in each corner. Suddenly Stephan's face turned white, and he quickly pulled out his phone to search for something online. He stared at the screen and shook his head, "Surely not!" He said shaking his head again in agitation.

"What is it?" Ellen demanded impatiently.

"Those are Hebrew letters!" he said dramatically tapping the corners of the card.

"I'm sorry, I am not making the connection. Why is this important?" she asked in confusion.

"Think about who else in the world would want to benefit from the knowledge Martin would have if he is where we propose that he is?" Stephan said with intensity glancing around him as if he expected someone was watching or listening.

"The Israelis," Ellen replied with finality suddenly remembering Martin's aggravation at the security delays every time he even accidentally had to pass through the country. He loved to visit the Holy Land but they certainly never trusted him given the other places he traveled.

"But who? How?" she gestured helplessly, "It couldn't have been Jack; he was in the hospital!"

They both looked from the card to each other's faces incredulously.

"Mr. Johnson? Surely not!" Ellen nearly laughed at how ludicrous it seemed. Even Stephan shook his head in disbelief. The problem was when could he have done it. Then Ellen remembered something vaguely, "Stephan, do you remember the night you came back to the Mission and had the nurse send me to bed?" There was only a slight annoyance in her voice. Stephan nodded.

"I went straight to sleep. I never went down and locked the office door after the nurse left me in my room. Well, early the following morning, I woke up from a nightmare because Char was growling. He chased someone down the stairs! I remember now. So much was happening I just assumed one of the crews or rescue personnel was wandering around." Ellen concluded sitting back in disbelief, she continued.

"He could have come back up here dressed as a firefighter or an EMT. I was out of it, and with all the people around; I would never have noticed!"

"If it was him, he has got to be one of the most incompetent agents I have ever met! Dropping something like this while searching someone's room, unbelievable!" Stephan shook his head. He was holding the card between his thumb and forefinger when Andrew walked into the dining room.

"So, you caught her with the ace up her sleeve, eh? Mother, I never would have guessed!" he chuckled giving her a quick squeeze. Ellen smiled weakly, and Andrew glanced questioningly at Stephan.

"Now what? Another revelation? Dad had a gambling addiction too?" his teasing tone broke some of the tension, but Ellen detected bitterness beneath his banter. She felt he was probably the most disillusioned by his father although he often hid it best. He picked up the card and flipped it over studying it more carefully.

"Is that Hebrew?" he questioned then stopped short. "Really? Are you serious?" He snorted sardonically. "Well, Dad always said they were watching him. So where did this come from; flown through the window by a raven or a dove?"

"Your mother found it in her room after someone had searched it," Stephan answered seriously, somewhat aggrieved by his banter.

"I'm sure there must be some other explanation." She sighed, slipping the card into her pocket as the door opened to admit James and Heather followed by a sleepy-looking Kate and a barely functioning Chris, whose eyes looked positively glazed. Pushing any significance of the playing card decidedly from her mind, she greeted her guests and talked for a moment about the blessings of electricity and their plans for the day. When Kate revealed she would be making a run to Taos to check out a friend's exhibition, Heather's eyes lit up with excitement.

After some discussion, they finally decided that Heather and James would accompany Kate and Andrew to Taos. James was hoping to catch a Hollywood producer friend at home at his ranch near there, and the chance to make that high-level of a contact was the opportunity that Andrew dreamed of in marketing his screenplays. After James and Heather had left to collect what they needed for the five-hour road trip, the family gathered for another goodbye. Richard had come in with Manuel, who he had been assisting with his morning chores.

Stephan and Chris would be flying back to Chris's NGO headquarters to arrange to travel as close as possible to the area where Martin had been going. All of the discussion ceased when Andrew suddenly stilled them with his hand raised, "What about Mom? There are probably people out there who are still looking for information." He explained to the others the playing card and the searched room. Richard cleared his throat replying in an annoyed voice,

"I am a big guy, and still you guys always forget I am here. My schedule is flexible; I can stay for another week. As long as I can check in with my research team regularly, they won't mind. There are several repairs that I can help Manuel with while I keep an eye on Mom."

Ellen smiled sadly to herself. Richard was right, not that she needed anyone to "keep an eye on her" as if she were an incorrigible toddler, but that while they never intended to, his siblings often ignored him. She had seen the hurt regularly throughout his childhood.

"We'll be fine." She said emphatically. "However, you must promise to keep in touch with me! I have no idea what is the most secure way to accomplish that, but I must know what is happening, Chris!"

Ellen saw the same look of anger and defensiveness she had seen so often.

"Ok, Mom! I will have someone from the office update you! Ok?" Chris responded, "I feel like I'm under the Mother's rules of occupation whenever Dad left." He deflated the barb with a slight grin.

It was true; she had always become more of a tyrant about keeping in touch when their father was gone.

"Hey, as long as you remember who you're dealing with, we're good!" She hugged him tightly, begging God inwardly to take care of him. She shook hands more formally with Stephan. After they had all gone their separate ways, Richard looked at her with a twinkle in his eye, "Stephan looks like the sort who could get lost in his own museum. Wonder if he knows he just hooked up with our version of Indiana Jones?" Ellen laughed for the first time in days.

She and Richard helped Rosita and Manuel clean up from breakfast then they sat down together at the thick carved kitchen table. Her beloved caretakers had heard bits and pieces over the past few days, but now the time had come to disclose all, for their safety as well, if there were more like Jack who would be coming.

She started from the beginning, telling of Martin's work, ministry, and their lives together, followed by the travel and the separations. When she told of his disappearance, the tears began to fall, not from her eyes alone. Somehow, even telling of her surrender to God in the chapel seemed easier with Richard there; he had always had a soft heart toward God. Ellen felt tremendous guilt knowing that she had been too absorbed in her own pain to help her children hold on to their faith. That her frustration had been a stumbling block to their relationships with Martin, or more importantly with God, was almost more than she could bear. However, with Richard even now, Ellen did not see any bitterness on his face, only compassion as he stroked Char's head and looked into her face.

As dispassionately as possible, Ellen told them what she perceived as the level of threat was from agents like Jack or even Mr. Johnson; although she still struggled to see him in the role of a highly-trained Mossad operative. Rosita's hand, which had been holding hers, tightened, and her eyes flashed. They decided they would each carry two-way radios to keep in touch. Cell phone service was still sporadic in some areas of the Mission compound. Manuel explained that since the irrigation ditches and field flooding had worked so well to prevent the fire's encroachment closer to the Mission, they had decided to repair and possibly reopen other old channels for further protection. This plan would keep them conveniently close to the Mission walls. Manuel intended to get as much labor as possible from the sturdy young man. Richard enjoyed the physical exertion and the companionship of one who could fill the space of the father figure he had so often lacked. After they had set off to work, Ellen returned to begin bringing order to the chaos of her office.

Even as she worked, she began compulsively to check her messages and email. Rationally, she realized that Chris and Stephan had only been gone a couple of hours, yet here she was, already falling back into the old familiar mindset that had marked her existence for so many years. Like a well-worn cloak, it slipped around her soul. As Milton wrote, "They also serve who only stand and wait." Through all the years while she had waited for Martin to come home, she had wondered if the mandate King David set up for his soldiers in the Bible story remained true. Would the share of the one who stayed with the supplies be the same as those who went down to the battle? Would God truly see the sacrifice of both and give them a similar share of the reward? Ellen's musings ended when she saw through the curved ironwork window a vehicle approaching the entrance to the Mission.

The insignia on the side of the expensive Land Rover heralded the nearby Apache owned casino. The passenger door opened, and a rather bedraggled Mr. Johnson struggled to extricate his suitcase from the back seat. Staggering slightly, he finally managed to handle his case and trudged head down toward the front doors of the Mission. Ellen sighed; definitely, this settled it once and for all. There was no way this pathetic little man was a highly trained Israeli operative. Opening the Mission doors, Ellen helped him with his bag and softly suggested a nice cup of coffee while Char sniffed his cigarette smoke infused leg and sneezed. Somewhat pitifully, Mr. Johnson shook his head saying that if he could just lay down until dinner, he would be fine. Gently, Ellen led him to his room where he fell across the bed without even bothering to remove his shoes. At least he did not appear to be drunk, just broke, and tired; the obvious result of gambling for two days straight without a break. Well, his room had been paid through tomorrow so he could sleep all day if necessary.

Ellen radioed Manuel that the guest had returned. Somewhat reluctantly, Manuel asked if she felt they needed to come into the Mission; he and Richard were making steady progress and were convinced that they could repair most of the irrigation channels. She assured him there was no immediate danger from the sleeping Mr. Johnson. Ellen could hear Manuel's excitement as he considered planting a field of sunflowers in the spring. Perhaps she should think about hiring more help for Manuel since there was so much he wanted to accomplish. This fleeting thought reminded Ellen of her neglected bookkeeping. Passing through the library after informing Rosita about the guest, Ellen paused. It had always seemed that Martin was closer in this room. As if, while he absorbed their contents, the dusty volumes had become infused with his spirit.

Absently, she pulled a book from the shelf and leafed through the pages of an English translation of a twelfth-century Iranian mystical poem. It had been vital to Martin to understand the stories of the people he met. "Building bridges for the message of God's love to cross over from one person or culture to another," could have been his motto. Shaking herself, she wiped a tear away with the back of her hand and sighed as she moved toward her office. When the waves of sorrow and despair rolled over her, she felt weighed down with the ache; as if, it was too much effort to try to keep her head above it all.

Sitting down at her desk to switch on her computer, she realized the book was still in her hand. A small plain business card slipped from the pages as she flipped through them. It appeared to be in Arabic script except for Martin's name, Dr. Martin Wright. Distracted again, Ellen tried an internet translator. The card seemed to be announcing a lecture by the "Ustadh"- the teacher of Philosophy. Ellen stared at the card wondering where and when this card had been used. There did not appear to be a date, time, or even a location listed. That was all there was, another dead-end.

A familiar frustration started to well up within her. It was the feeling of being excluded, marginalized, from the life of the man who had insisted that he had loved her. One who had taken a marriage vow till death do us part, and then had parted from her continually. In spite of his travel, he had always managed to provide for their needs financially. She had no complaints there. Even now, she could not have purchased or renovated the Mission without the funds provided by his life insurance. If he was alive and miraculously returned, how would she ever manage to pay it back?

Jolted by this thought, Ellen remembered why she was sitting staring at her computer screen. Bookkeeping was a chore for her even though she was an organized person by nature. She thrived on routine and desired order. Martin had always insisted that he did too, but it would have been impossible to deduce that from the chaotic life he had chosen to live. Maybe he intensely desired order and control at home because of that very fact. He just never was able to tolerate the chaos that the children brought into his "private" life. Still, they loved him. Strange how children never seemed able to let go of the hope that their parent would become the person they knew they should be.

They were out there now, determined to find him if humanly possible. How much time from their lives could they seriously afford to dedicate to this? Richard's research committee was more interested in final results than weekly progress reports. Chris would be technically going under the auspices of his organization, so he could continue to make inquiries discreetly. Kate was more or less a self-employed artist now that her husband had finished his nursing education and was working, but he would not be willing to live without her for long. Andrew was still waiting for his big break and writing from home freelancing and taking care of his little daughter while his wife worked. A long separation was just not tenable for them either. Ellen shook herself; she had to get control before her negative thinking dragged her into the pit of despair. It was a well-worn and slippery path whose landmarks were all too familiar.

Her eyes fell on Martin's worn copy of *My Utmost for His Highest* by Oswald Chambers she had kept in her office. She looked up the date, March 6. *...in much patience, in tribulations, in needs, in distresses* — 2 Corinthians 6:4

"When you have no vision from God, no enthusiasm left in your life, and no one watching and encouraging you, it requires the grace of Almighty God to take the next step in your devotion to Him... It takes much more of the grace of God, and a much greater awareness of drawing upon Him, to take that next step than it does to preach the gospel. Every Christian must experience the essence of the incarnation by bringing the next step down into flesh-and-blood reality and by working it out with his hands. And the only way to live an undefeated life is to live looking to God."

She had spent the last two years looking away from God. Could she look at Him now? As the old song said, could she "turn her eyes toward Jesus, look full in his wonderful face"? She thought again of the crucifix as she had seen it in the chapel on the night of the fire. Moreover, how could she even take the next step if she did not find a way to look to God? Living in a void as she had been doing, she had existed without that constant connection. Chris and Stephan were heading into danger; she had to trust God again. Only now she had to overcome the fact that she had trusted Him with Martin and look what had happened! But then again, he might still be alive, in which case God had taken care of him. However, he was being kept from her...why? Was she so detrimental to him that God was compelled to keep them apart?

Char brushed his nose against her leg blessedly interrupting her tangled thoughts. Ellen let him out through her office and then the front doors of the Mission. As she stepped out, she saw Char bounding joyfully over the softening snow toward Manuel and Richard, who stood at the edge of the valley examining the fire-darkened hillside. Ellen leaned back against the sun-warmed side of the Mission wall.

For the first time since the fire, she was able to absorb the extent of the devastation. The fire had stripped the mountainside of its covering leaving it naked, erasing its forest-robed hills, and blackening its rocky bones beneath the ashes. In a couple of months, brilliant green grasses fed on the charred richness of the scorched soil would cover the stubble of stumps on the face of the canyon. Beauty would come from ashes. Ellen struggled to remember the rest of Isaiah's scripture. Did it not also promise the oil of joy would replace mourning? Perhaps only in heaven.

Char was barking excitedly and bounding toward her as Manuel and Richard followed carrying something. Richard was cradling a large speckled bird he had wrapped carefully in his jacket. Roadrunners were not as common in the mountains as on the desert floor. This one appeared to have been attempting to out-run the blaze until he had reached the safety of the flooded section of the valley floor next to the Mission. Traveling across the flat desert roadrunners can often reach twenty miles an hour, but he had apparently been caught on the steep mountainside where running to escape was nearly impossible. His feet looked badly scorched, and his feathers appeared singed also; however, she was glad Manuel had tied a piece of cloth over his eyes to calm him. His beak still looked decidedly vicious.

Ah Richard, Ellen smiled, her heart warmed by the sight of his gentle care for the wounded bird. Always he had wanted to save the helpless creatures of the world. Inside the kitchen, Richard held the bird, which was about the size of a long-legged skinny chicken, while Manuel treated and bandaged the burns covering its feet and legs. There was no help for the singed feathers; they would eventually molt and make way for new. Since Roadrunners typically chase down their prey of insects, rodents, and snakes the singed feathers did not disable the bird, but the badly burned feet definitely did.

Manuel retrieved a cage that he had used for Char when he was a puppy. They gently placed the bird within and wearing gloves removed the covering over his eyes. He clacked bravely and stumbled on his bandaged and obviously painful feet, but he appeared genuinely grateful for the bits of meat they offered him. Char seemed determined to smell test the creature in his former pen and received a sharp nip on his nose as a reward. For his pathetic whining, Manuel chided the offended dog gently in Spanish as he daubed disinfectant on the bite. Keeping a wary eye on his protagonist, Char happily soaked up the sympathy his wounded pride deserved.

The distraction of dealing with the singed bird and the offended dog was welcome to Ellen. Anything was better than the hypnotism of the clock while you waited for someone's return. Occupation was always the best diversion. Idle hands might not be the Devil's workshop, but if one had both an active imagination and a tendency to melancholy, an idle mind could certainly be his torture chamber.

Chapter 7

Around eleven pm, Ellen heard the crunch of the gravel as the group returned from their excursion to Taos. When Ellen led the way to give them some refreshments in the kitchen after their long hours on the road, the bandaged roadrunner was the immediate center of attention. Andrew and Kate had seen them before but rarely this close. Heather and James were both from east coast cities, so they were ecstatic to have this close encounter with the unusual creature. They all laughed at Char, who still gave the vicious beastie a wide berth choosing to survey it from the opposite side of the room. Not wanting to disturb Rosita, Ellen settled them at the kitchen table with sandwiches, cheese, and fruit while they told her of their adventures.

The trip appeared to have been useful in building some close friendships, as well as, an opportunity for establishing contacts. They had found Kate's friend Dirk's exhibit, where he promptly dropped to one knee and proposed to Heather. According to Kate, this was his typical first greeting. James was frowning, and Heather was blushing slightly; although embarrassed, she couldn't quite contain her smile. Dirk had accepted his rejection with a sardonic smirk, after which they had enjoyed his show and the shops nearby. Ellen could tell from Andrew animated expression that his encounter with the producer must have gone well. The producer was interested in filming live coverage of James on a Middle Eastern concert tour for a documentary. The tour would include stops in Dubai, Saudi Arabia, Kuwait, Jordan, and finally Turkey.

Ellen held her breath; fearing what was coming next. Andrew explained that he had been invited to accompany James and write the narration for the documentary. It was a fantastic opportunity! Exactly the break he had been anticipating so long. Ellen kept the smile pasted on her face even though she felt her stomach tighten with dread. Still bubbling over with excitement, they filled the kitchen with laughter and plans until James and Heather retired for the night. Ellen turned from the sink where she had retreated to wash the dishes after hearing their news. Andrew and Kate studied her face.

"It will be ok, Mom. I have been waiting forever for an opportunity like this one! James is the sort of person I think I can collaborate with easily. And primarily, it's fully funded! Once I sign the contract and have the check, Celina can stop working and be home with Sylvia while I am gone. It is what she has always wanted! This is exactly the job that I have been looking for; I just cannot turn it down." His eyes gleamed with excitement and promise.

"I'll take that nice professor picture of Dad and me together. If I just set it up in my room, maybe if someone takes an interest in it, I can make some discreet inquiries. At the very least, I would be on the right side of the world to fish Chris out of trouble!" He glanced at Kate, who rolled her eyes.

"Anyway, I want to talk to Celina before it gets any later- give her the news!" He squeezed Ellen's shoulder briefly and hurried eagerly from the room.

She met the serious eyes of Kate, who spoke softly but matter-of-factly, "Don't discourage him, Mom. It's his first really big break! He's not Chris. If anyone is capable of discreet inquiries, it's Andrew. If anything, he's too cautious."

"I know he has worked hard to find an opportunity like this; he deserves this chance! It's just that part of the world is so unpredictable. If something happened to him, I mean, he has a wife and little girl too." Ellen paused sighing then continued. "Well you found your friend's exhibit, what did he say?"

"You mean after he had proposed?" she snickered raising an eyebrow. "Seriously, he has done it to me so many times that Josiah has given up threatening his extermination. So, Heather was anxious to escape him after that, which gave me time to talk to him. He loves a challenge, so he was very excited! He said something about sneaking into Los Alamos labs and using their equipment." She laughed at the look of horror that passed over Ellen's face.

"It's ok Mom if he tries it, he will pull it off, no worries." She grinned as if breaking into the National Lab to analyze a photo that the authorities wanted to confiscate was no big deal. A non-conformist to her very core.

"He will figure it out. He can't stand a mystery. Besides if he lacks insight there are always the mushrooms!" Kate chuckled wickedly.

Char crept surreptitiously to Ellen's side and leaned against her leg, warily keeping one eye on the evil bird. Ellen silently rubbed his head as if to smooth away her dread. Surely, her sons were not diving in to save a drowning man and themselves about to be pulled under; however, this was not the ocean depth, but the desert's shifting sand. It might even be quicksand. She sighed deeply, looking up into Kate's sad eyes. Growing up with three brothers and an often-absent father, Kate had become good at hiding what she felt even from Ellen. This fact made the vulnerability and aching sadness visible now on her face even more heart-wrenching.

"What if it's like Stephan said; what if he went there willingly? And now, what if it's not that he can't return; it's that he doesn't want to come back?" Kate's question hung heavily in the air.

Somehow, hearing the exact commentary that had been rattling around in her head spoken aloud comforted Ellen. As if the fact that someone else was thinking the same thing gave her thoughts credibility. Also, the feelings behind Kate's words carried with them the same loss and abandonment she felt as well. It just tasted like a betrayal.

"I guess if that's what he has done, he would surely have a good reason." She replied. Ellen had grown to hate pat answers that were supposed to be comforting. Her words sounded with a tinny hollow even to her ears. She had to give Kate more to hold on to than that lame expression.

"He wouldn't leave the work if people were responding, I am certain of that. If he felt like what he was doing was making a difference and saving lives, he would not leave them until they were safe or he had someone to take his place. Even for us."

"He wouldn't abandon them, but he would us," Kate spoke with bitterness.

"He never thought of it as abandoning us. It was almost more that we were part of him; his self, so that if he denied himself, he denied us also. We were just part of the sacrifice package, I guess." Ellen rubbed her tired eyes. These moments when Kate was willing to share were so rare she must stay alert.

'You know, sometimes when I need advice, I find myself thinking that I'll wait and ask Dad when he gets home.' Kate said wistfully wiping away tears with the back of her hand.

"Well maybe you'll still get a chance," Ellen thought, but would not say. There was no way she was going to raise Kate's hope; instead, she reached across the table and clasped her hand.

"You seemed so strong-willed and opinionated that he was always a bit amazed when you did ask." She squeezed her hand gently. "Sometimes he thought your ideas were profound; it was just your communications method that he struggled to comprehend."

Kate gave her mother a watery smile, "Bah! Who needs punctuation and proper spelling? Yeah, my thoughts were so profound that he would offer to pay for a theology degree. Surely profound thoughts were wasted on an artist. What would I ever do with them?" She sighed heavily and stood up stretching which caused the roadrunner to begin clacking a loud warning that sent Char scurrying to the doorway.

"Char! You are ruining your fearless-guard-dog reputation." They could not help laughing at his sheepish expression.

"If only Jack had known that roadrunners were dog repellant he might have used a different tactic in his attempts at intimidation," Ellen mused as they walked down the corridor to Kates room.

After hugging her goodnight, Ellen wandered out into the courtyard to sit on the edge of the stone fountain. The Milky Way stretched across the sky brilliantly luminous in the crisp night air tinged with the lingering smell of an extinguished campfire. Martin had so loved the night sky of New Mexico. The miles of wide-open space and the absence of light pollution made it seem that you could see every star in the universe. The sky glittered alive in a dazzling display, a deep blue darkness scattered with celestial diamonds.

"The heavens declare the glory of God." She quoted softly.

"And the firmament shows his handiwork," a sad voice intoned from the darkness.

Ellen jumped to her feet and whirled toward the sound. She laid her hand on Char's neck feeling the hair raised and his body tense when Mr. Johnson stepped out of the shadow of the arched corridor. Seemingly unaware of startling her, he strolled over to sit on the fountain with his face turned skyward. He sighed deeply without taking his eyes off the sky.

"Yes, we also have that in our Tehillim; Psalms for you."

Ellen lowered herself to the fountain edge stiffly.

"So, you are Jewish?" She asked attempting to speak casually.

"Yes, and the playing card was mine." He said it so matter-of-factly Ellen looked sharply at him while he continued to gaze at the stars.

"I don't think you are going to invite the police to cart me away for breaking and entry, especially since I didn't take anything. I am assuming the photo in question is gone?"

"Why I should tell you anything!" Ellen demanded incredulously. "You came here under false pretenses, to violate my privacy and steal!" How did he even know she had found the lost card? Did he have the place bugged?

He kept his eyes on the sky and said half-heartedly, "We're on the same side; war on terror and all that. Either we find him and get the information we want, or he gets blown up by a drone while he's talking to the neighbors." His words were even more chilling for the stark lack of feeling with which he spoke them. He just seemed tired. Maybe he had been sharp and dangerous once, but now he seemed deteriorated and dreary.

"Why are you doing this?" she asked.

"Doing what?" he asked petulantly. "I haven't done anything yet!"

Ellen did not miss the "yet".

"This investigation, job, assignment, whatever you want to call what it is you people do; you don't seem overly committed to it. If you don't really want to be here, why not just call it quits and go home?" Ellen was growing angry, sincerely hoping that he would just leave. This game had too many players already.

"I promise to be my intimidating best as soon as I recover from the shock of losing nearly a year's income to the local natives." He lowered his eyes from the sky and hung his head pathetically. Ellen still almost felt sorry for him, rather than frightened. Was this an act? It certainly seemed to throw her off her guard.

"Look I don't have the photo or anything else that can help you find him, or I would have used it myself long ago." There was finality in Ellen's voice.

He sighed heavily, "So what do I have to do to get you to tell me where the photo is? Tailing all your children will take some time. Or we could just forget the picture; wait him out, and either they will kill him, a drone will get him, or we will grab him as soon as he leaves that area."

It was Ellen's turn to sigh, "In reality; it doesn't change anything, does it? He's been dead for two years."

"There are those who would be more willing than I am at the moment to put pressure on you and your family." His voice held an ominous warning.

"Why?" Ellen retorted with increasing hostility. "You all seem to know where he is; if he is still alive! What more could you possibly hope to gain by threatening us! Remember, we all assumed he was dead!"

"We might be able to identify who of our enemies are with him in the photo, for starters," he replied.

Ellen hoped he was not gaining enthusiasm for his investigation. She stood up attempting to see his face in the darkness.

"I do not have it, and neither do any of my children." Ellen was relieved she could answer honestly. "Your stay with us is finished tomorrow, Mr. Johnson. I'm sorry if you wish to extend your visit; I'm afraid we will not be able to accommodate you." Ellen turned and walked stiffly across the courtyard to her office door. To her relief, she found Manuel waiting in the shadows there. When she unlocked her door, he followed her inside.

"He might be more of a threat than we thought," Manuel said with concern.

"Maybe, but he leaves tomorrow," Ellen spoke with determination.

He would not be the only one leaving; Kate would be taking Andrew, James, and Heather to the airport. Then, she hoped to be able to connect with her friend Dirk and get some answers regarding the photo. Ellen was not worried about Mr. Johnson attempting to follow them to Albuquerque. It was not as though you could secretly follow someone on the wide-open high desert road to the city when you could see for fifty miles and often only met one or two other vehicles. Maybe he would just give up and wait it out as he said. Ellen shook off her annoyance and made the arrangements necessary for the following day. Manuel nodded in agreement, but Ellen could tell he was far from at ease about Mr. Johnson.

The next morning when Ellen said goodbye to Heather and James, it was evident they would remain friends with each other definitely, but also with her family. She offered them discounts for all the upheaval they had endured in their stay, but they refused, insisting on paying the full amount. Andrew's eyes shone with excitement for the adventure ahead, so Ellen forced herself to swallow her feeling of foreboding and joined the animated enthusiasm of the young people. She hugged them all, exchanging contacts and demanding that Andrew update her on the tour whenever he had access to the internet.

"Sure Mom, but after I have talked to Celina and Sylvia, ok? I intend to keep in touch with my wife first!" he said it intensely, and Ellen caught the accusation again. He had always judged his father harshly for the extended periods of silence.

"Just be careful," She said into his jacket as she hugged him tightly. "I can't go through this again!"

"I'll be surrounded by people; worry about Chris!" he said lightly, but his eyes were serious. As she waved them goodbye, an expensive, sleek Mercedes passed them as it crept up the driveway.

A very chicly dressed Mrs. Johnson emerged to glare at her coldly. Ellen lead the way to her office where Mrs. Johnson stridently claimed the discount offered before stalking back to her still running vehicle. Manuel was depositing a miserable looking Mr. Johnson's bag into the trunk. As he opened the car door, Ellen could already hear the sharp stinging tones that seemed to cut through the morning air.

"How much did you lose?" She was shrieking, "You stupid a-", the rest of the word was cut off by the slamming of the car door. Ellen could see his shoulders hunched as if enduring a sudden downpour to prevent the torrent from smacking him in the face. Ellen turned away shaking her head, no matter how sinister he had seemed in the darkness last night, she still felt sorry for him.

She and Manuel turned and walked quietly to the kitchen with Char at their heels. For the first time in a week, the Mission felt peaceful. Ellen breathed deeply, drawing in the fresh fragrance of the clear mountain air. She was thankful there were not many guests for next week. They could all collectively use a breather. In the kitchen, they found Rosita smiling as she watched Richard feeding the road-runner, who seemed to be adjusting to the idea of handouts quite readily until it saw Char. Then it lifted its comb and began to clatter and clack fiercely. Char hid behind Ellen until he could reach the relative safety of the opposite side of the large granite countered kitchen island. From there, he kept a wary eye on the foul crea-ture while he ate his breakfast.

Ellen had not expected Richard to say goodbye to the guests or even his brother. Goodbyes had always been difficult for him. He looked up pensively from the bird and asked what time she thought Kate would be back from Albuquerque. That was his other "thing", time. It had always been "what day/what time will Dad be home." Of course, he missed his father, but he missed them all. He suffered from the family separation more than the others did. They had often teased him that he would have them all living on a commune together in the backwoods of Canada. He would just smile; because it was true.

Ellen laid her hand on his broad shoulder, "I'm not sure; sometime tonight if she can find her friend quickly".

"Or if she doesn't get lost," Richard grinned. Kate's sense of direction was legendary for its failures.

"She's got her cell phone," then it was Ellen's turn to grin. "If she has it turned on."

"If it's charged, or not already slid under the seat," He continued. "At least she can't blame it on her cat, or poor Josiah."

Ellen laughingly explained her daughter's phone trials to the amused Manuel and Rosita as they sat around the kitchen table for breakfast. After they had finished eating, Manuel picked up a tattered, ancient looking Bible and read Psalm 5. (RSVCE)

¹Give ear to my words, O Lord; give heed to my groaning.

² Hearken to the sound of my cry, my King and my God, for to thee do I pray.

³ O Lord, in the morning thou dost hear my voice; in the morning, I prepare a sacrifice for thee, and watch.

⁴ For thou art not a God who delights in wickedness; evil may not sojourn with thee.

⁵ The boastful may not stand before thy eyes; thou hatest all evildoers.

⁶ Thou destroyest those who speak lies; the Lord abhors bloodthirsty and deceitful men.

⁷ But I through the abundance of thy steadfast love will enter thy house, I will worship toward thy holy temple in the fear of thee.

⁸ Lead me, O Lord, in thy righteousness because of my enemies; make thy way straight before me.

⁹ For there is no truth in their mouth; their heart is destruction, their throat is an open sepulchre, they flatter with their tongue.

[10] Make them bear their guilt, O God; let them fall by their own counsels; because of their many transgressions cast them out, for they have rebelled against thee.

[11] But let all who take refuge in thee rejoice, let them ever sing for joy; and do thou defend them that those who love thy name may exult in thee.

[12] For thou dost bless the righteous, O Lord; thou dost cover him with favor as with a shield.

Ellen realized when he stopped reading that she had closed her eyes and tears were running silently down her face as she prayed the words from her heart. If only He would spread His protection over them all and cover them as with a shield, surely, they would return safely. They joined hands and Manuel began to pray in Spanish. The room seemed filled with the warm breath of faith, and Ellen felt wrapped in the comfort of a loving embrace. Even the bird had settled, and Char rested his head on her knee in satisfaction. It almost seemed sacrilegious to break the moment.

However, they must prepare for the next week's arriving guests. Chiefly, they needed supplies. Manuel and Richard would go down the mountain to Alamogordo where prices were lower than in the local village. After assembling the list, the two men took the truck so that they could collect the horses on their return. Rosita began cleaning the dining room, great room, and library while Ellen started in the guest rooms. When she stopped in Richard's room to leave some towels, she smiled at the chess set on his desk. He always seemed to have a game going with someone either physically or online. She wondered who had been playing this game with him. Just for fun, she played a move.

Kate's room was chaos. Ellen sighed, she would have straightened it, but that had always gotten her in trouble.

"You move my mental sticky notes; then I can't find anything!" Kate had frequently protested when she still lived at home.

Ellen stood up the photo of Kate and her mountain man Josiah that was lying on the nightstand. Ellen wished that he could have come. In many ways, she and Josiah understood each other, since they had quite similar personality types. Maybe that was why he was a source of stability and comfort to Kate; somehow, he responded to her the same as Ellen would. She chuckled to herself; she had never heard of a girl marrying someone like her mother, and undoubtedly Kate would not appreciate the observation.

Moving on to clean the room Chris had occupied, she was not surprised to find things discarded under the bed. Yes, of course, there would be socks. This guy needed to get married. When Ellen opened the drawer of the bedside table, she found a tattered photo. Ellen sat on the edge of the bed looking at the face of the one girl that Chris had never really let go of, at least from his heart. She was a beautiful young Asian woman, whose more traditional parents had struggled to accept what they saw as an irresponsible American boy. Ellen hoped there was no deeper significance to Chris leaving the picture behind for this adventure.

In Stephan's room, Ellen looked around for something out of place. She shook her head; he must have been in the military at some point. Everything was certainly ship-shape ready for the white glove inspection. In true military fashion, lying on the desk was a neatly scripted envelope bearing the message, "to be opened in the event of my death". Like a good soldier, was he leaving behind his last will and testament before going into battle? Ellen pocketed it unopened along with Chris's picture.

Mr. Johnson's room smelled of stale cigars even though there was no smoking allowed, and Ellen propped the door open to let in some of the crisp mountain air. Char took this as his invitation to enter and sniffed around the room until he latched on to something under the bed. Ellen took it from him and discovered what appeared to be a key holder of the type with a car unlock button. Ellen wondered if it belonged to the big black Mercedes that his "wife" had brought to collect him. No doubt, he would hear about it if it did. He did not seem dangerous even to her now, just slimy somehow. Maybe it was the gambling. The few times Ellen had entered the casino; she had left feeling depressed for the desperate individuals who seemed to lose even their sense of self-preservation in their greed. She pocketed the key fob and left the door ajar to freshen the air as she moved to the next room.

In Heather's room, to her tremendous delight; she found lying on the chest of drawers an intricate pencil sketch of Char. Her talent was portrayed beautifully by the way Heather had seemed to capture the soul of her faithful companion. The thoughtfulness of the gift was an accurate illustration of the sensitivity of the artist.

Ellen still did not know what wound had brought Heather to the refuge of Wayfaring Mission; perhaps the love she had found here in James would last and bring healing. Ellen added the sketch to her growing collection, beginning to feel that she must be on a treasure hunt.

James had left a schedule for the middle-eastern tour in his room for which Ellen was very grateful. The itinerary would give her actual dates and locations so that she could track Andrew's progress through the region as he accompanied James. The tour did not begin for another two weeks, but it would take that long to make all the preparations. Even getting a visitor visa for some of the countries on the tour could take weeks or even longer without some high-level intervention.

Ellen made her way into the chapel to sweep and dust. Time seemed to stand still as she moved from pew to pew, feeling more as if she were caring for something living rather than cleaning religious remnants of a bygone age. Without thinking, Ellen knelt in front of the crucifix at the altar. It seemed like months instead of days since the night of the fires. Now instead of facing the surrender and loss of herself and Wayfaring Mission, she confronted the surrender and loss of her sons. This time, did the suffering servant understand? Perhaps only God the Father who sent his son into danger could comprehend the fear and dread her heart carried. Ellen clung to the altar until her knuckles were white begging God for mercy and protection. She must leave them there, leave them to God. Trust Him.

Still, it came again, could she trust the God who had taken Martin and even if he were alive had not returned him? Did she have a choice? Would she live in tortured fear and dread of what God might allow or believe that God is good and loves them more than she could? Ellen said the words, committing them by force of her will even as her heart cried out in fear. The Lord gives, and the Lord takes away; blessed be the name of the Lord; Job had said. Abraham had brought his Isaac. Now in the stillness of her own heart, Ellen brought them both, these sons who had seemed most distant from God since the loss of their father. Would He consume them in the sacrifice or would God himself provide a ram?

Chapter 8

The familiar rattle of the old truck and horse trailer meant that Richard and Manuel had returned, hurriedly Ellen wiped her face and went out the chapel doors to meet them. They were busy unloading the horses when Richard caught sight of her face. He came toward her leading her horse.

"Is everything all right?" he asked anxiously.

"Everything is fine," She replied, but did not look him in the eye; rubbing the neck of her big gray quarter horse. Manuel joined them.

"Carter said you could come and take care of his horses for him later rather than accept payment now," Manuel said. Ellen smiled at the idea. Living in the southwest had taught her that people did not usually collect on debts like this one. Carter accepted that she would be there for him if he needed help, so there was no need to talk about payment.

Ellen was relieved to set about unloading supplies and not to have to be subject to their scrutiny. Just as they were sitting down to dinner, at the thick wooden table in the warm glow of the golden and turquoise accented kitchen, Kate walked in followed by a middle-aged man with unruly black hair, sharp dark eyes, a thin mustache and a goatee.

"Oh great," Ellen thought ruefully, "Dirk is a gypsy pirate." Kate had always had a weakness for the type. To Ellen's chagrin, he walked toward her and clasped both of her hands in his.

"Kate never told me you were beautiful! Would you please consider marrying me?" he said in a melodious voice with only a hint of playful pleading in it.

"No thank you, been there, done that!" Ellen said fervently, but she could not help laughing. He winked at her and immediately turned to Rosita.

"I don't think so Amigo!" Manuel interrupted before he could even get started.

Dirk sighed dramatically, "It never hurts to ask; someday someone will say yes."

Kate patted him consolingly on the shoulder and motioned to the seat closest to the Roadrunner. After the simple grace that Manuel offered, Dirk looked rapturously at the table laden with burritos, Spanish rice, green chili stew, salsa and tortilla chips, delightedly clapping his hands together he declared, "If this is how the righteous people eat, throw away my stash, and dunk me in holy water, I'm signing up!"

His enthusiasm disturbed the roadrunner who had been intently surveying the group from his cage who chirruped, clacking his beak loudly and dramatically behind him. Ellen had never seen anyone turn completely around and jump up on a chair in a single movement before that moment. She would have sworn every hair on Dirk's bushy head was standing on end. Good grief, no wonder the man felt the need for calming remedies; he was a bit high-strung! Through their laughter, they explained the presence of the wounded bird in the kitchen. Dirk was finally able to calm himself enough to sit normally, though he still kept a wary eye on the caged Phoenix as he named it exclaiming, "I thought the Devil had heard my declaration and had come for me at last! Aren't road runners supposed to beep-beep?" turning to glare at Kate, who was laughing so hard tears filled her eyes.

"You did that on purpose!" he protested. "Trying to scare me straight?" With effort, she controlled her spasms of laughter.

"No more sneaking up on me when I am alone in the studio at night!" she remonstrated.

"I shall never again!" He declared, "I plan to hire on here as chief cook and bottle washer for the rest of my days just for the food!" helping himself to a big, meaty burrito.

Throughout dinner, they told the story of "Phoenix", now named, and Kate went further explaining the frequent pranks of their guest. The opportunity to laugh and forget her troubles for a moment was like a balm to Ellen's weary spirit. It seemed impossible to keep from smiling at Dirk's flamboyant rhetoric and enthusiasm. Ellen wondered how Kate's somewhat calm and resolute husband, Josiah endured Dirk's exuberant friendship with his wife. Her fears were relieved when Dirk had followed Manuel and Richard to the great room while she and Kate helped Rosita with the cleanup; Kate leaned back against the counter as if she had deflated, "That guy is exhausting! He's so high strung it's like trying to have a conversation with a cartoon character stuck in fast forward." She laughed weakly, "I feel like the coyote that has been chasing the road runner all day long!"

When they had finished cleaning up and had taken the tray with steaming mugs of chocolate into the great room, they found Manuel, Richard, and Dirk gathered intently over an ancient looking chessboard Martin had salvaged years ago from Burma.

"Ha!" Dirk shouted, and he moved his knight with a flourish. Ellen saw the gleam in Richard's eye at this display. She had seen that look before; Dirk should just give it up now. Two moves later, the game was over with Richard as the obvious winner. Dirk determined to drown his sorrows in his chocolate, and it did seem to have a calming effect.

Having drained his cup luxuriously, he slipped a pair of curator gloves from his pocket before gingerly removing the now carefully wrapped photo from its sleeve of high-quality paper. Placing another paper under it on the table, Dirk looked up with a slightly accusatory glance.

"Do you have any idea how many fingerprints I found on this? Mine did not need to be added to the collection." By this time, they were all hovering over the photo, but he motioned them back dramatically.

"Every breath leads to further decay!" For all his chaotic appearance, he seemed to take his work quite seriously.

"First of all, obviously, this is a digital image that has been printed on high-quality photo paper. So, it did not come from some remote village with little to no electricity. This fact leaves out most of the country where you say this photo could have originated. Whoever printed this, did so in a major city where there would be access to high-quality equipment as well as paper. My guess would be somewhere in UAE, Saudi Arabia. It was a not a cell phone but a camera which was not of the best quality, so the image is not too clear. However, it appears they captured the image while the vehicle was moving, one would assume, over rough terrain so that could also account for the lack of clarity. You can see this from the blur out the back window. My guess would be dust or sand raised by the vehicle, which suggests dirt road, no pavement. Obviously, he is not in a jungle or anywhere else where there is vegetation. The clothing of the men, as well as their headgear, suggests they belong to a Syrian tribal group, where their sympathies lie in the current conflict, I cannot tell. Their weapons are the typical passed-on hardware from any number of military invasions in the countries of the region." He paused and looked into Ellen's face while the full weight of his words pressed upon her soul.

"However," he continued, "I see no evidence that his hands are restrained, and their weapons do not seem to be threatening him as much as they are just being held ready for action. I have enlarged his face on another print so you can see if it is possible to identify." Again, he removed a carefully wrapped print and laid it before her.

There was no way to identify the top half of the face covered by the blindfold, but the beard below it left no doubt. It had to be Martin. Ellen let out the breath she had not realized she was holding in a slight sob. Still, this could have been taken on some earlier trip, not within the last two years.

"Is there any way to determine how long ago the picture was taken?" she asked somewhat huskily.

"From the condition of the print and what I would assume is rather a rough handling; I would determine no more than a year old. Although that does not indicate when the picture was taken," he added quickly, "just that it was printed within the last year. It could have been taken a couple of years even before it was printed."

"Is there anything else you can tell us?"

"Not much, I'm sorry. However, I have enlarged the faces of the other men and attempted to clarify them as much as possible for purposes of identification. Will you be releasing the photos to the authorities then?" he asked with caution in his voice.

"No, we will be investigating using our sources. We have not found the authorities particularly helpful in the past." Ellen answered guardedly.

She stared intently at the enlarged photos; there was something about one man's face. In some way, it seemed recognizable. Frowning, she shook her head. Dirk immediately responded, "What is it?"

"Somehow it seems I have seen this face before." She said pointing to the man sitting on Martin's right side.

"Well let's hope not personally," Dirk answered eagerly, his eyes gleaming. "If someone were able to hack into the CIA's face recognition database, he would find this to be a tribal leader in a predominantly Taliban-held area. Not that anyone would risk doing such a foolhardy thing!"

Ellen thought he looked positively gleeful.

She sighed, "Risk hacking the database or risk entering that area?" she realized her voice registered her hopelessness.

Impulsively, Dirk gripped her hand, "The fact that your husband was with this person and was still alive in this photo, also according to Kathleen, there have been no demands. He has not appeared in a prominent execution video, and the feds are still snooping around, all this means there is still hope!"

Ellen smiled at him weakly, wondering after this stream of observations exactly how much Kathleen had told him.

"So, how long until they catch up with the guy who hacked their database?" She asked him with smiling accusation.

He squeezed the hand he was holding gently, "You're worried about me, aren't you?" he grinned slyly. Ellen released her hand and shook her head at him. The man was incorrigible! He carefully collected the artifacts and handed her the folder. Ellen looked at it in her hands, unsure even where to keep it. What if more Jack-type agents arrived? She was surprised when Manuel softly asked if she would like him to "put it away" for her. Relieved, she nodded, handing him the parcel. If anyone could find a hidey-hole in the place, it was Manuel.

Suddenly, she felt deflated as if the new information only added weight to the pressure that seemed to be crushing her. Manuel and Rosita swung into action, herding the others to their rooms, clearing, and straightening. Ellen wandered into the library switching on the recessed lighting. Unhurriedly she walked around the walls trailing her hand over Martin's books, looking at his face appearing in the photos around the room. She had not realized she was crying until she sank into a chair and dropped her wet face in her hands. Char whined and licked her face gently. She wrapped her arms around him and wept into his soft fur.

When she had wept herself dry, she moved into her office to switch on the computer. Messages waited from Chris and Andrew. Chris and Stephan would be flying out soon and would be traveling for days before they would reach the border where they would join their colleagues and continue overland. Mentally, Ellen estimated that there would be approximately a week before she must face those long gaps when there would be no information. She remembered well the blackout days with Martin. What had been his last message? Probably, "Love you the most today". It had been a kind of game with them to see who could text the message first. He loved competition; she loved hearing from him. Then it stopped. She waited, and the plane crashed. That had seemed the end, and then it was not. Almost certainly, he was dead even if he had not been on that plane.

Sighing, she checked Andrews's email, which brimmed with excitement for his upcoming assignment with James. Somehow, James had been able to expedite their visas, and they would be leaving at the end of the week. At least he would not be out of internet contact even if they monitored his messages. He had included his flight itinerary so she could follow his progress. Ellen looked at the list of cities, knowing only too well the dangers that existed in each place. Sighing, she shut down her computer and after locking her office climbed the stairs with dragging feet.

While undressing, she discovered the small key fob in her pocket. She would have to look up Mr. Johnson's address to send it to him. She noticed the pinpoint battery light was shining brightly. As she set it on the nightstand, Char sniffed it suspiciously, before he lay down on his rug beside her bed.

Ellen awoke as she did every Sunday morning to the sound of the chapel bell as it echoed its clarion call through the valley. Unlike most Sundays, since she came to the Mission, Ellen did not view it as simply as a break in the monotony of her everyday routine. This time she wanted to be there; she felt drawn to the sacred place. As was their custom the elderly ladies arrived for mass early, making their small procession into the chapel. Manuel conducted the liturgy in a mixture of Latin and Spanish, so when Ellen slipped quietly into the sanctuary, her participation was limited since she was not Catholic and understood only a few words.

However, sitting listening to the words of faith, even in another language connected her to some deep place within her spirit. "God is spirit, and those who would worship Him must do so in spirit and truth". Besides, since her travail the night of the fire, Ellen felt bound by a kinship with these elderly grandmothers. When she clasped their frail hands and looked into their wrinkled, kindly eyes, she saw a depth of understanding that can only come from those who themselves have been to the valley, walked through its dark and terrifying recesses with nothing to hold on to but the hand of faith. Ellen was confident Wayfaring Mission had been preserved through the years by the prayers of these saintly supplicants.

To her surprise when she got to the dining room after the service, Dirk was already busy eating. That he was devouring large quantities of food was not surprising, that he was awake so early was. It seemed that as long as he could eat continually, he would not need sleep. Dirk announced that, with her permission, he would continue at the Mission as a paying guest, if not as a family friend. After some cheerful, good-natured wrangling, they decided he could remain as volunteer staff for as long as he wanted to help. Seeing the quantity of food he consumed at breakfast, she considered renegotiating. How did the man stay so thin? By midday, it was apparent he consumed calories by sheer nervous energy.

Saying goodbye to Kate tore at her soul leaving her feeling fragmented. She could not tell them so, but every time one of her children left, it was as if a section of her being went with them, leaving her diminished. Still, it was not fair to keep Kate away from Josiah; she had experienced firsthand the high cost of separation on a marriage. As always, Kate sensed her loss.

"Sorry, Mom," Kate said with tears in her eyes. "He doesn't do well on his own."

Apart from the time that Josiah spent working at the hospital, he and Kate were never apart. They had each other and felt that was enough, at least for now. Ellen often felt guilty for Kate's aversion to the idea of having children. She worried that in her pathetic attempts to parent them by herself, without much engagement from Martin, she must have scarred her children for life or at least put Kate off from any desire to be a mother. So instead of changing diapers and washing baby bottles, Kate did commissions and painted canvas, building her portfolio instead of a family. Ellen hugged her tightly; Kate was as close as she had to a best friend unless Char counted, but it was time to let her go. After all, Kate was leaving her with this manic, gypsy hacker, what more could she want. Ellen sighed.

Apart from Dirk, there were not many guests scheduled for the week. The skiing season was nearly over, but the heat that would later drive the residents of the high deserts to seek refuge in the mountains had not yet arrived. Under normal circumstances, guests arrived on Monday morning, but Ellen had made an exception for a young woman named Anna, and Nadie her four-year-old daughter, who were driving from Canada and were uncertain how long their journey would take. They arrived in a dusty four-wheel drive almost at dinner time. Ellen thought they looked Native American, but not from the Apache tribe she was most familiar with in the area, more like the Navajo.

Over dinner, they discovered Anna was a substance abuse expert from Calgary, a member of the Tsuut'ina tribe, who had come at the invitation of the Mescalero Apache tribal leaders to offer some assistance in setting up a more holistic addiction recovery program. The loss of traditional lifestyles and culture, combined with the sudden influx of revenue from the casinos, left many young people confused and vulnerable. There seemed to be no place for them either in the traditions of their tribe or the white man's world.

Her dark haired sober-eyed daughter, Nadie seemed particularly fascinated by Richard watching him intently throughout the meal. His various attempts to smile, make faces, or converse with his limited understanding of her language were met with somber consideration, but little other acknowledgment. She kept this guarded reserve until Char slipped into the kitchen for his dinner and received his nightly chastisement by Phoenix, the recovering roadrunner. To Ellen's surprise, Nadie did not seem alarmed by its loud protestations, but instead scrambled quickly from her chair and ran eagerly through the doors toward the sound. The adults followed and found her squatted down at eye level before the agitated creature. Rapidly, she spoke to her mother in their language. For the first time, Ellen saw a slight smile cross Anna's face.

"She says this is a noisy prairie chicken. Her father was a conservationist who was attempting to reintroduce the species to Canada. He was killed by a drunk driver last year." She looked away as her voice seemed to falter. As she was speaking, Richard jerked upright from his squatting position.

"I'm sorry, but was his name Charlie Lightstar?" he asked with alarm.

"Yes," she answered sadly.

"I... I knew him...we had exchanged some research. I had no idea! I am so sorry!" he stammered with shock and alarm.

Anna only nodded and looked away from the intensity of his gaze.

"It's been hard for Nadie." she murmured.

Gently, Richard knelt by the small girl and began to tell her the roadrunner's story even attempting a few of his limited supply of words from her dialect. After a couple of minutes, Nadie slipped quietly onto his bent knee as she studied the bright-eyed bird. Only Ellen heard the mother's sharp intake of breath and saw the sadness in her eyes. She reached out to get Richard's attention, but Anna shook her head. Finally, after Richard had placed a glove on Nadie's small hand and allowed her to feed the sharp-beaked bird, she turned with glowing eyes and spoke again to her mother. Anna smiled and held out her hand. Somewhat reluctantly, Nadie rose from Richard's knee and returned the glove. Gravely, she bade Phoenix good night and then just to be fair to Char, who licked her cheek causing her to wrap her arms even tighter around his furry neck. She glanced back at Richard and waved shyly as her mother led the way to her room. A look of painful sadness passed over Richard's face.

"Now I understand how Stephan must have felt," he said passing his hand over his eyes.

"How so?" Ellen asked.

"I sent Charlie the research projects that kept him on the road. It didn't even cross my mind that he might be married or have a child. I'm no better than Stephan." he shuddered.

"I did not know about them; because I never asked. Then one day, I couldn't reach him anymore, so instead of investigating, I just assumed he had drifted away; lost interest in the project. I feel horrible! Maybe I was the reason he was on the road that day!" he struggled to control his emotions.

Ellen laid her hand on his shoulder saying, "There was no way you could have known, son! You were not responsible for the drunk driver. Charlie must have loved his work, or he wouldn't have taken on the projects. I'm sure he appreciated the fact that you valued his opinion."

"Maybe, but I enabled him to live like Dad; absorbed in something that took him away from the ones who needed him most. I, of all people, I should have known to ask. Instead, I used him for the information he provided, and when he disappeared, I didn't even bother to find out what had happened. Instead, I was annoyed that I had lost a resource." Richard sighed deeply and walked out into the night.

There was no way she could protect Richard from the weight of the guilt he felt, but this was a tremendous load to carry, and the hurt that surfaced in connection to his father seemed only to heighten the pain. She knew Martin had never understood his influence in the lives of his children. He assumed that if he was not physically present in their lives, he had little effect upon them. Now, he would never know how much impact his absence had left.

Ellen remembered a brief time in their lives when they had kept foster children. She had always been shocked at the intensity of the longing the children had for a relationship with their missing parents. The parents had not done well in caring for their children, which was why they were in the system. Still, the children never stopped hoping, longing that their parents would become what they knew they should be. It was a mystery how children who had been so deeply wounded in their relationships could even have a concept of a good parent. Perhaps deep within imprinted on our souls we all carried the fingerprints of the Father God indelibly marking us with the impression of what love should be.

Chapter 9

When Ellen came into the great room, Dirk was studying the chess board and sipping his hot chocolate. He looked up when she entered. Ellen did not realize that in her agitation from her conversation with Richard, she was distractedly fingering the key fob she had taken from her pocket.

Dirk reached out his hand, "may I look at that?"

She handed it to him explaining she had found it in Mr. Johnson's room and would need to mail it to him. Dirk examined it carefully and then began walking distractedly around the room inspecting every nook and cranny.

"This is going to take too long!" he spoke with exasperation as he rushed out of the room to return at a run a few minutes later. He took a small electronic device from his pocket and began circling all the while clicking the key fob. Having covered the great room, he entered the library and continued the same procedure.

"Aha! Got you!" he shouted running into the room with a small black box and rushing to open the laptop he had brought with him.

"It's a recording device! All we have to do is download the data, and we will know what he knows!"

Ellen stepped back flooded again with the increasingly familiar anger of intrusion and insecurity.

"So, all I have to do is access the files in it…" Dirk said completely absorbed in his task. "Transfer the recorded files… and we're in business!"

Ellen shuddered when she heard her voice playing back in that disembodied way from the speakers in Dirk's computer, realizing it was word-for-word her conversation with Stephan. The recording continued even after they had entered her office. Somehow, the listener had even been able to increase the range. As if experiencing some method of extreme immersion therapy, Ellen began shaking as she relived every moment. Seeing her pallid face as she grasped the chair back, Dirk abruptly stopped the recording.

"When does it end? She asked faintly.

Dirk looked momentarily perplexed as to whether she was referring to the ordeal in general.

"What is the last recording?" she said more steadily.

Rapidly Dirk forwarded through the files. With angst, she realized as she listened, that he had recorded everything except Dirk's conclusions regarding the photo. She had already found the fob at that point and had apparently unknowingly shut it off. So, the listener had every detail of the plans Andrew, Stephan, and Chris had made. No doubt his agency would now be dogging their steps as well. Ellen dropped her head in her hands feeling the throbbing of her temples. There was just no end to this. Well, there was nothing to do now but warn them. She turned back, "Would he have been able to access this data even after he left?" she asked, the weariness evident in her voice. Dirk examined the device and searched its capabilities online.

"I'm sorry; yes, I think that as long as he has a computer, he would be able to receive it wirelessly. The fob was just a remote way to turn on and off the recording to save battery. They can even access your cell phone to record, but as the coverage here is sketchy; I guess they decided to use something more traditional. I hate to be the bearer of more bad news, but it's safe to assume they are also monitoring all your email and social media accounts."

Ellen had no social media accounts; since her desire in coming to the Mission had been to escape the rest of the world. However, with dismay she realized her only contact through email to Andrew and Chris was now compromised. It seemed pointless even to warn them; since Mr. Johnson or whoever was listening already knew all their plans. Feeling overwhelmed with the futility of it all; Ellen dragged her feet up the winding staircase to her room. These days she was either dropping from exhaustion and troubled dreams or unable to sleep at all as her mind raced from one eventuality to the next. Beside her bed lay the last gift Martin had given her before his disappearance, a new study Bible. She opened it and began to read, "Unless the Lord watches over the city, the watchman stays awake in vain. It is in vain that you rise up early and go late to rest, eating the bread of anxious toil; for he gives to his beloved sleep." She so wanted to believe and trust that the Lord would watch over them tonight and that she was the beloved one who could sleep.

She eventually drifted off to sleep although the outlines and forms of listening people invaded her thinking. When she awoke to the early morning sun, she felt sore. Her muscles were tight, and she felt the tension of a headache beginning. Coffee. By the time, she passed through the dining room she was surprised to see Anna and Nadie already eating. She had forgotten that they were on a child's schedule. Ellen realized with relief that as usual, Rosita had everything prepared. No matter when the guests arrived for breakfast somehow, it was always ready.

She greeted them, but Nadie was more interested in Char. She followed Char to the kitchen where she insisted on serving him his dog food herself. She would have attempted to feed Phoenix also, but Ellen refused; requiring her to wait for Richard or Manuel. Reluctantly, they returned to the dining room, Ellen with her coffee and Nadie watching the door impatiently. Anna tried to interest her in completing her breakfast but to no avail. When Richard finally walked through the door, looking rather worn himself, Nadie bounded out of her chair and grabbed his hand. Somewhat startled, Richard still smiled allowing himself to be lead to the kitchen to supervise Phoenix breakfast.

"Nadie seems to love animals," Ellen commented as she finally sat down with her coffee.

"Like her father," Anna said softly.

"I'm very sorry for your loss. I do understand." Ellen replied gently. Anna looked down nodding slightly.

"What does Nadie do while you are working?" Ellen inquired. "I mean; we wouldn't mind if she wanted to stay here with us during the day." Ellen tried not to sound too hopeful. It was just the presence of a child seemed to brighten the entire atmosphere.

Anna was about to respond when Nadie emerged from the kitchen holding tightly to Richard's hand. She spoke something to Nadie, who looked up at Richard and then led him over to the breakfast counter and proceeded to do the best she could to fill his plate for him. It seems he was in the category of creatures that needed feeding as well. When he sat down, she sat beside him willingly accepting a muffin from him and munching contentedly together with him.

"I'm sorry; whenever he was home, she was her father's shadow. I guess she feels comfortable with you." Anna apologized to Richard, looking embarrassed.

"No problem, I don't mind," Richard smiled sadly in sympathy for the little girl's lost attachment.

"I suggested that Nadie stays with us today. We could take care of her, don't you think?" Ellen asked hopefully.

"Uh… sure," Richard said looking at his mother with some uncertainty.

"Rosita and I wouldn't mind a helper." Ellen offered by way of reassuring Richard that she did not expect him to babysit.

Anna examined Richard for a long moment before turning to speak to Nadie in her own language. Nadie replied rapidly, smiling pleadingly and looking from Richard to her mother. Anna questioned her sharply and spoke sternly to her. Ellen thought she could recognize the "you better be good" speech in any language. Nadie lowered her head and with many gravely spoken, "Yes Momma's" appeared to be winning the debate.

Finally consenting, she gave Ellen her contact information and instructions on how to reach her. Ellen was surprised that the casino was hosting Anna's substance abuse sessions. Curious, Ellen asked why she had not taken a room there. Anna confessed that a full suite was provided as part of her contract. Looking around the room and then at Nadie she continued, "I wanted more of a home environment for Nadie. The air in the casino seems polluted by smoke and greed." Nadie was still munching her muffin and slipping Char pieces under the table whenever she thought no one was looking.

"She seems to have made herself at home here," Anna smiled genuinely.

After her mother had left, Nadie wandered into the kitchen where she was soon happily employed stirring, fetching, and generally getting in the way. All the while, Rosita chatted cheerfully to her, delighted to have her company. Nadie did not say much, although she too was evidently enjoying herself. Seeing that she was occupied, Ellen was about to slip off into her office when a rather bedraggled looking Dirk walked in rubbing his eyes and headed for the coffee pot.

"Did you manage it?" Richard asked conspiratorially. Over a long swig of strong black coffee, Dirk gave an almost imperceptible nod.

"Of course," he answered smugly. "The only problem is that it took me until 4 am," he added yawning mostly for emphasis. Richard grinned at his mother.

"When Dirk told me about the listening device, we thought it was only fair to give them a bit more than they expected when they try to access the recordings."

"Sent them my own personally developed, baaad bug," Dirk said cracking his knuckles visibly quite pleased with himself. "That should keep them occupied for a while."

Before Ellen could protest at the pointlessness of provoking their adversaries, the door opened, and Nadie's dark little head poked out. Seeing Dirk, she spoke to him rapidly in her language, and to their surprise, he answered in kind.

"Where did you learn to speak that language?" Richard asked amazed as if the gypsy man had acquired the gift of tongues overnight.

"Unfortunately, during one period of my life, I spent a considerable amount of time in the company of OxyContin users. The most generous suppliers of which came from this little bambino's people group. That is why her mom's work is so important; it is a very real problem in her tribe." Dirk responded with guilty acknowledgment.

Meantime, Nadie assumed that it was her job to wait tables and was gingerly balancing the plate she had piled high for Dirk. Fortunately, Manuel who had come in behind her managed to help her steady it to the table. She smiled up at him but quickly moved to sit beside Richard.

"What's up?" Richard asked looking at Manuel's expression.

"We may need to have Winchester's right foreleg checked; it appears to be swollen. He may have gotten kicked at Carter's place."

Dropping her horses into an established herd even for a short time meant there was often a pecking order adjustment. As a gelding, Winchester was not aggressive which made him an easy target.

"I'll go with you," Richard responded immediately but stopped when he stood only to find his hand quickly imprisoned by Nadie. He looked in bewilderment from her to his mother. Dirk came to his rescue rattling off a question in Nadie's language. She only shook her head smiling coyly and grasped Richard's big hand in both of hers.

"Sorry Rich," Dirk laughed. "You have been taken prisoner by the visiting tribe!"

Ellen saw his consternation, but also his delight. Surely there was no danger as long as Manuel was there to supervise. Unlike his older siblings, as the youngest child, Richard had very limited experience in the babysitting department. After they all had helped with the breakfast cleanup, and the babysitters and their charge had left, Ellen stood outside while Char took his morning walk with her back against the Mission's solid wall. She breathed in the morning's freshness thankful for the brief moments of respite. She returned to the kitchen to pick up another cup of coffee and was passing through on her way to her office when she noticed that Dirk was still lounging in the library.

"Oh, I thought you had tagged along with the others," Ellen looked at him quizzically. His expression looked serious, which was not a typical response from him.

"Weeell" he said drawing out the syllable. "I realized last night about 3:30 am, right after I had hit send to infect and debilitate the computer system of an oper-ative from an allied nation," he paused for breath. "That I might need to hear the whole story."

"Please remember that I did not ask you to do that," Ellen said reproachfully. She sighed. He was in pretty deep, and she was not sure at this point whether he had jumped or been pushed. Instead of sitting down, Ellen paced around the room. Did she trust him or not and did it even matter? With resignation, she started from the beginning telling him their story. Pacing back and forth, she handed him various photos related to phases of their life. Their meeting in college, the early years of struggle, Martin's time as a university professor, his final ac-ceptance of the call of God, and the beginning of his years of travel. Finally, she sat down with resignation sighing, "The last photo you know. You have seen it and if you listened to the recordings; well, there's not much left to tell," Dirk cleared his throat and leaned forward, "That doesn't explain why he was there. I am a very long way from a nationalistic American, but why would anyone go into this area willingly?" his tone was not accusing, just questioning.

"I cannot give you a satisfactory answer to that; you would need to have known him. He felt his first allegiance was to God. He used to say that if we had obeyed Jesus last command to go into the entire world to preach and disciple, then these people would not be our enemies now. He wanted to build bridges using the "Isa", Jesus, of their scriptures to show them the more excellent way of love, not hate. He also felt a tremendous responsibility to the Christian nationals who live in these areas and daily face the reality of persecution and death for their faith. If he felt he could help them, he would go." Ellen grasped the curved iron bars at one of the windows feeling flushed and agitated.

"The thing is… He was good at it! He could go in and out of those places without drawing attention to himself. The authorities only discovered him when, apparently, he did not die on the flight that crashed. The only reason he is a person of interest now is that he might still be alive staying in that area and, of course, the men in the photo." She ended with despair dropping her head against the cool iron bars. Finally, as if remembering he was still there; Ellen turned at looked at him seriously, "The reality is that no one who does not share his same passion for God will understand his actions."

"Do you?" he asked softly.

Ellen swallowed the lump in her throat. Did she? Surely, she ought to be able to put herself aside and see God's purpose and plan were greater than her own desires. Could she reach the point of trust where she could say God had worked all things together for good to those who loved Him and were called according to his purpose? Only by the grace of God.

"Someday I hope I will." Her voice did not sound hopeful. Dirk looked down silently at his hands clasped before him. Finally, he spoke somewhat self-consciously, "I had never known people with real religious faith until I met Kate and Josiah. The way I grew up, as a carnival brat, life was all about superstition, magic, luck, and taboos. Kate and Josiah aren't perfect, but they have something, and they love each other so much. When I first met them, I tested them, to see if they would condemn me to hell fire for my heresies. I even tried to stir up trouble between them, which did not work, and they never changed in the way they acted toward me. They were nice to me in spite of myself." He looked embarrassed at his admission.

"So, when she asked me to analyze the photo, well…except for consultations in a professional capacity, no one had ever trusted me personally before; I wanted to help."

"And now?" Ellen asked sadly.

"Now it seems even more strange that someone would make this kind of choice! It seems like he must be crazy, a fanatic, to leave everyone who loves him to go to people who would hate him. Even want to kill him! Was he some kind of maso-chist, a wannabe martyr? How could he do that to his family?" he said almost angrily. Remembering something, Ellen replied, "Hold on a minute." Retrieving Martin's old copy of Oswald Chambers, she turned to a well-worn page saying, "This was one of his favorite writers." She read aloud, "If we obey God, it is going to cost other people more than it costs us, and that is where the sting comes in. If we are in love with our Lord, obedience does not cost us anything; it is a de-light…If we obey God it will mean that other people's plans are upset, and they will gibe us with it, 'You call this Christianity?' We can prevent the suffering; but if we are going to obey God we must not prevent it, we must let the cost be paid…Stagnation in spiritual life comes when we say we will bear the whole thing ourselves. We cannot. We are so involved with the universal purposes of God that immediately we obey God others are affected. Are we going to remain loyal in our obedience to God and go through the humiliation of refusing to be independent, or are we going to take the other line and say- I will not cost other people suffering? We can disobey God if we choose, and it will bring immediate relief to the situa-tion, but we will be a grief to our Lord. Whereas if we obey God, He will look after those who have been pressed into the consequences of our obedience. We have simply to obey and to leave all consequences to Him. Beware of the inclina-tion to dictate to God as to what you will allow to happen if you obey Him."

"The writer of that, died when he was forty-three years old leaving his young wife and a two-year-old daughter. Most of his work was compiled and published by his wife after his death." Ellen sighed

There was a minute of silence while the words seemed to hang in the air, and Dirk stared at the floor frowning.

"Well, did that happen? Has God looked after you?" he demanded.

"Well yes, He has given me Wayfaring Mission and provided ways for my chil-dren to move forward with their lives. I guess it is just that the loss and pain have taken longer to heal. Now, this mess has ripped open a lot of scars." Seeing his doubtful look, Ellen continued, "I am not sure that the lack of healing is always God's fault. One has to be willing to cooperate with the process. I guess, you also have to be prepared to accept that the healing could come even if all the questions are not answered, and things don't turn out the way you want." Ellen looked down at her watch. She handed the book to Dirk.

"This book pretty well sums up the principles that guided Martin's life. Maybe it will help you understand. As far as your personal involvement in all this, please do not feel obligated in any way! If you are having regrets, feel free to walk away at any time. It is one thing for our family to take risks, but we have no right to ask you to do so."

"And not see how all this turns out? Are you serious? I am the kind of guy who reads the last chapter first! I gotta know the ending!" he returned with a measure of his former bravado.

Ellen moved through her office to open the heavy entrance doors for Char to have his morning walk. She leaned against the thick walls that even now were absorbing the solar warmth of the bright sun pouring through the brilliant blue sky. Somehow, her conversation with Dirk and hearing the words Martin had doubtless given his life for seemed to strengthen her. Maybe God had been there for her, was here even now. Ellen left the entrance doors open as well as her office door, so Char could return when he had finished his walk.

Chapter 10

When she logged on her computer, there were messages from both Andrew and Chris. For the first time since she had received her last email from Martin, Ellen noticed that she received multiple copies of the same email. Martin had explained that each time an email was being checked; when it was scanned for flag words or someone read it and then sent it on, she would receive another copy. That meant that the email from Chris had been stopped twice and the email from Andrew in Dubai four times. Ellen wondered if it would matter if she warned them that whatever they were sending was not secure?

Andrew had arrived in Dubai and was staying with the concert crew in a very luxurious hotel. He reported total exhaustion from jet lag, so he had ordered something in his room rather than going to the restaurant. When room service delivered, they insisted on setting the table. One of the visibly foreign workers, Andrew guessed Filipino, saw the picture of Martin that Andrew had set out, and began talking rapidly to his co-worker. His friend shook his head in embarrassment or fear, but at his colleague's insistence turned to Andrew and asked shyly, "This is Dr. Wright? You know him?" When Andrew affirmed that Martin was his father, both young men came to him and clasped his hands.

"We have been so worried…He came and spoke to our group…Is he all right…we have not heard from him?"

Their comments and questions tumbled over each other, and Andrew had to focus to follow their accents. Finally, he was able to ascertain that Martin had come to speak to their small gathering of believers and kindly had helped several of them by contacting their families in the Philippines for them. He had even helped them financially during emergencies. They had become concerned when he had left and not returned. Andrew was hesitant to tell them that he was presumed dead. Suddenly, they turned to one another speaking rapidly in Tagalog and then told Andrew that they must give him something. Naturally, he was dying with curiosity, but he had too much work to do now to speculate. Promising to notify her as soon as he had found out the mystery, he ended his message.

Even though the message was not bad news, Ellen sat back with tears in her eyes. Martin had loved the foreign workers, especially the Filipinos that he had met around the world. Since, like them, he also spent so much time away from his home; Martin felt he understood to some degree the great sacrifice they made working in foreign countries to send support home to their families. He often said those working in middle eastern countries faced the worst hardships.

In her limited travels with him, she had frequently seen him slip money into the hand of the hotel maids, cleaners, and other service personnel. He was a generous tipper, but this was always something more, just for them or the needs of their families. Often, they followed him out when he left, some of them with tears in their eyes for his kindness. She remembered that he was also actively organizing safe meeting places for the workers for fellowship and prayer. Maybe one of those seeds planted along his way would bear fruit now.

Chris messaged that since he and Stephan had reached an area with little internet availability and would have limited opportunities to message her. He did report a strange incident. One of the armed guards, who was traveling with their convoy carrying humanitarian aid into a refugee area, had a picture on his phone taken with someone who looked like Martin. Ellen remembered again how often young men had wanted to have their pictures taken with him. She assumed it was both respect for his position as a professor, and his distinguished white beard. Chris continued that he was waiting to ask the guard until he could find someone he trusted to translate their conversation. He also expressed concern for Stephan, as he was well aware that the refugee situation they were entering was going to be an intense emotional overload for an inexperienced person. Ellen only hoped the "old soldier" was still buried under the philanthropist somewhere and would surface if need required.

Ellen had become so engrossed in the messages that she did not register the sound of the approaching vehicle and was not brought back to reality until she heard horrendous barking, and growling! Running to the open entrance, she discovered Char had backed someone against the wall of the Mission and was aggressively refusing to let him escape. Under the bandages and in spite of his casts, Ellen recognized the malevolent glare of Jack Smith! She grasped Char's collar and commanded him back to her side. Dirk too had sprinted out the door and was eyeing the scene with jaw dropping astonishment.

"I demand you return my belongings!" Jack's voice sounded gravelly and was menacing when he spoke, even if his battered appearance was not. He gestured violently toward Char with his good hand.

"And keep that son of a bitch away from me, or I'll kill him!" he threatened loudly causing Char to snarl more intensely and to show his teeth.

"How did you get here?" Ellen started to ask and then saw a local policeman leaning against his patrol vehicle. Strangely, the officer appeared to be taking no notice of the proceedings. Ellen walked over to him and greeted him.

"Officer, this man brought a firearm onto my property although the Mission visitor packet clearly states that no guns are allowed on the premises. He claims to be a federal agent and, therefore, felt he could confiscate some of my private papers without any legitimate warrant. He was attempting to leave with those papers on a stolen 4-wheeler when he was caught in a slide off the mountain. I would be happy to return his firearm to you if you escort him off my property." Ellen spoke as calmly and dispassionately as possible throughout her explanation.

Still leaning against his door, the officer removed the toothpick he was chewing and with a lopsided grin answered in a slow drawl, "Yeah, he tried to pull all that federal officer stuff on me too. I let him 'commandeer' my vehicle and me to drive him up here, but I am afraid this is not a local law enforcement issue, so that is about as far as I am willing to go." He winked. "Your dog doesn't seem to like his look much either."

"I'll call my dog off so Mr. Smith can get back to your car, and I'll bring his belongings out," Ellen grinned back at the young man in gratitude. He walked with her to the place where Char stood his ground with hackles raised and rubbed his furry head.

"Tell Manuel whenever he is ready; we will let him train our canine force." Then he ambled over to the cursing Jack and taking him by his unbandaged arm led him protesting loudly back to his vehicle. When Ellen returned with Jack's belongings, she could still hear his steady stream of profanity directed at her, Char, the officer, and any other entities within shouting range. She shook her head and handed over the emptied gun and small travel bag. Graciously, the officer signed a receipt for the incapacitated Jack in spite of his verbal abuse. When they drove away, taking the rough road none too gently, Ellen noticed that the officer had lowered his car window and was playing some country music, very loudly.

Ellen turned around shaking her head in disbelief at what had just occurred only to find Dirk leaning against the wall, doubled over laughing so hard he was holding his sides. Before long, she was laughing too. Although deep in her heart she doubted that this would be the last time she would encounter Jack or his kind, she was thankful he was out of the way for now.

Straightening and gasping for breath, Dirk managed to say, "I know who that guy is! I have run into him before doing forensic work for the feds. Such an arrogant Jacka..." Dirk either caught himself cussing or was laughing too hard to continue; Ellen was not sure which. She called to Char, who still was agitatedly pacing the end of the driveway as if to ensure that the offensive person was gone. She soothed and petted him and led the way into the Mission where this time she closed the heavy doors.

Not long after, at the sound of the truck and horse trailer returning, the already agitated Char started barking again. When Manuel stepped from the cab and heard the sound of barking, he sprinted to her office. Seeing his alarm, Ellen quickly explained the situation that had just occurred, and unlike Dirk, Manuel did not laugh. He did soothe and calm Char speaking softly in Spanish as he stroked him. By the time Nadie and Richard had made their way to them, Ellen was happy to see Char's tail thumping gently as he eagerly licked Nadie's face. She giggled and protested but still held tightly with one hand to Richard. He seemed to have accepted his new attachment, and grinned saying sheepishly, "Well, I guess we won't need to wash the ice cream off after all."

Ellen shook her head in mock disgust and led Nadie to the kitchen to wash her face properly and to let her help with lunch. Over lunch of green chili cheeseburgers, chips, and salsa, followed by Mexican wedding cookies for dessert, Dirk regaled the others with the story of Jack's visit. In spite of themselves, they were soon all laughing at his colorful retelling. Still, Manuel was uncertain, "Perhaps we had better work more closely to the Mission for a while." He said seriously causing Ellen to recall the reason for their absence.

"How is Winchester?" she asked.

"Quite a nasty cut but nothing truly damaged, just sore," Richard replied.

Suddenly Nadie turned to Dirk and launched into a long soliloquy. Dirk leaned closer and concentrated on what she was saying while the others waited patiently.

"Well, I caught some of it." He said sitting up. "The horse's leg was hurt, the Dr. had good hands, like 'Daddy Richard's," he smirked at Richard's embarrassment. "Then the big dog was angry cause the bad man was here, and the bandage needs to be changed on the strange prairie chicken." Dirk paused and looked up.

"How does she know all that?" he asked amazed.

"Maybe," said Ellen with frowning emphasis, "She understands more English than she can speak so we might want to watch what sort of stories we tell around her."

Dirk was only slightly cowed, "I meant how did she know about the roadrunner?"

Curiosity got the better of them all, and they trooped into the kitchen to see the bird. In his desperate attempts to remove the bandages, Phoenix, the roadrunner had nearly managed to mummify himself. Dirk looked at the small child with a mixture of wonder and suspicion while Richard and Manuel set to work releasing and redoing the bird's bandages. It chirruped and clattered but found the extra bits of meat more than acceptable and when restored fluffed and flapped its singed feathers. Whether the Roadrunner was attempting to restore its dignity or order to its plumage, Ellen was unsure.

Char might have been willing to take Jack down, but the bird was a bit too much for him, so Helen mercifully took him with her check on Winchester. The big gray quarter horse leaned over the gate of his stall to nuzzle her pocket where she always had a carrot or apple. Not having grown up with horses as Martin had, riding, and even being around the large animals had intimidated her when they first met. Martin had tried to teach her to hold with her knees and guide the animal as he did, but she always felt she was bouncing around wildly and causing both she and the horse pain and stress. It was not until she had come to the Mission and had worked with Manuel gentle tutelage that she had learned to trust herself and at least this particular horse. There had not been much time for Martin to share his interests and enjoyments before life seemed to move them in separate directions. She toward the children and him away; he always had seemed to be going away. Ellen leaned her head against the broad neck of the big horse and sighed.

As she walked to her office, she saw that Anna had returned and was sitting with Richard on the edge of the fountain. Nadie was excitedly dancing up and down, twirling, and describing her day's adventures in childish chatter. Richard looked embarrassed, but he smiled when Ellen greeted them and passed by to her office. She wondered if Richard might seize the opportunity to follow her and escape, but he did not. In fact, even though they moved into the great room as the temperature cooled the couple continued their conversation.

It was not until after dinner that Ellen had an opportunity to get back to her computer to check for messages. Once again there were four copies of the email.

Andrew' message read:

"So, after all, the rehearsals, set up, interviews and filming when I finally managed to get back to my room to write; I heard a knock at the door. It was one of the guys I had spoken to about Dad. You'll never guess what he had in his hand! Dad's black bag! He said the day Dad left to fly to wherever he went; he bought a smaller more portable bag. He did not want to leave this in the hotel safe since he did not know when he would return, so he asked the leader of the group he met with to hold it for him. I haven't had time to go through it thoroughly, but it looks like he took only the bare essentials. Medicines, passports but the rest are still here. Even his old laptop and iPad! I am charging them now, but knowing Dad, his technology will be obscurely password protected so we may need Kate's kooky friend to hack them for us. The hard part is that it probably means he left for wherever he was going with only the necessities. That's all, for now, must get some writing done. Love you!"

The notorious "black bag"! Martin had never gone anywhere without it; although she often teased him in later years that he needed a smaller purse. He believed in being prepared which meant it was always heavily packed, and he never left it behind. Ellen switched on the lights and wandered around the library looking at the photos. There it was, perpetually slung over his shoulder like an extra appendage. Somehow, the thought that he might be out there somewhere without it pained her. As if, as long as he had his bag he would be shielded; protected somehow. It did not matter that her thoughts were illogical, even superstitious.

Ellen swallowed the lump in her throat and wiped the tears from her eyes. She must be falling apart, for two years she had not shed a tear now she was blubbering over everything.

The thought of being able to see what was on his devices was hopeful and somehow unsettling, like viewing a ghost. Still, Ellen felt excited by the prospect. Her excitement shriveled as fear reached its icy fingers around her heart when she saw the following cryptic message from Chris.

"No chance of going farther! Everyone is pulling out, and we may have to also. The reports from that area are horrific! Beheadings, crucifixions, and brutality, even to children that are beyond belief! I may not be able to find a working internet connection again. If he is still in there, it is too late; he will already have been killed. If he managed to escape, maybe I will hear something in the camps. Everyone is just focused on their own survival, not much hope for news. I love you, Mom! Please pray for us!"

The last line spoke more to Ellen of his desperation and fear than his descriptions of the nightmare he was witnessing on the faces of the refugees. Chris was not sentimental in his relationship with her or toward God. Desperate anxiety seized her; if only he would just come home now! Martin was already lost to them; she just could not face losing another. Unfortunately, she realized that even if he received her desperate plea to come home, he might not be able to get out now, provided he could bear to leave those so desperate for help.

Intentionally living so remotely, she had isolated herself from news of the rest of the world. There had been no reason to care what was happening once Martin was gone. With trepidation now, she clicked on a news page and be1gan to read the horror of this terrorist group's rapid rampage across the countries where Martin had so often traveled. Hopelessness and dread tightened their vice grip until she could scarcely breathe. Char whined and licked her hand then quickly left to return with Manuel. When he saw her ashen, grief-stricken face, he crossed himself then steadied her with his arm around her while he looked over her shoulder at what she was viewing.

"Ten piedad de nosotros Dios!" he spoke in anguished prayer.

Somehow, Ellen managed to click back to the message from Chris and gesture mutely for him to read. Manuel's rough, warm hands closed around her trembling ones, and he began to pray. For a full minute, Ellen did not even register the sound of him speaking. The words were only background noise to her racing heart and the roar in her own head; however, as he continued, she felt the reality of his words reinforcing her soul, surrounding her as with a shield of faith. Facing this new threat, she had no hope for Martin or Chris but in God alone; that was her new reality.

When the last sweet benediction dropped from Manuel's lips, Ellen was startled by the small chorus of "Amens" that surrounded them. Anna and Nadie crossed themselves, and she realized Richard's hand was on her shoulder. Even Dirk slipped quickly from the doorway with what looked suspiciously like tears in his eyes. Through her tears, Ellen looked from one concerned face to another. There seemed no way for them even to comprehend the danger sweeping toward Chris and Stephan.

Little hands clutched hers as Nadie climbed into her lap. She laid her small soft cheek against Ellen's chest and wiped her tears gently with tiny fingers. Something about holding the warm little body close and feeling her innocent comfort melted the icy hold that fear had taken on her heart. God loved her son just like He loved this little one. That immense love of the Father in heaven was so much greater than even the love she had for Chris or Martin. He would have to save them, or He would allow them to be taken home to Himself. Either way, they would never be out of His arms; He would hold and comfort them.

"Oh, thank you Nadie! You have made me feel so much better. I was very scared, and you have given me courage. I know God will be with them no matter what happens." She finished brokenly hugging the small form to her heart.

With a catch in her voice, Anna translated Ellen's words to which Nadie nodded her head vigorously. She responded with a stream of words and clapped her hands excitedly. Reluctantly, Anna explained that she was excited that if they went to see God, they could meet her Daddy also. Brushing aside Anna's hasty apology, Ellen smoothed Nadie's dark hair and kissed the top of her head. She couldn't speak, but her soul accepted the trusting faith of the child as her own. She would believe that this trauma, even if it meant death, would not be the end.

Feeling her mission accomplished, Nadie scrambled off Ellen's lap and grabbed Richard's hand dragging him off to check on the Roadrunner. Anna watched them wistfully for a moment then crossed to Ellen and held her gently. The sisterhood of sorrow embraced them, as a multitude of wives and mothers have held one another while pain and loss lashed and bonded their souls in unifying grief. Through the mingling of tears, women throughout the ages have forged the steel for soul survival.

Chapter 11

The next few days seemed a blur to Ellen. She performed her tasks automatically, numbly. Some hidden part of her soul was clinging to God, yet her conscious emotions seemed dormant, cocooned deep within, and safe from further harm. She seemed barely aware of those around her who looked at her blank expression with obvious concern. She obsessively checked new outlets for information regarding the advance of the terrorist army. Day after day, stories of horror emerged, but there was no further message from Chris.

When anxiety and fear, nightmares and sleepless nights threatened to overwhelm her, Ellen made her way to the chapel. She felt a renewed kinship with the elderly ladies who kept their vigil during the fire. Char slept many nights at her feet while she knelt hanging on to the altar as if it was her lifeline. The war raging against this threat was a different sort of fire, but none the less deadly for its sweeping destruction. Often as he made his rounds, Manuel would find her kneeling or face down before the altar, and he would spend some time praying with her. While his words and faith brought comfort, Ellen prayed that the Spirit who could interpret the deep groanings of her heart would respond when she had no words.

Finally, a message came from Andrew that they were wrapping up production in Dubai, and he would bring the black bag with him and meet his wife and daughter at the Mission. He had writing to finish, and he might as well do it there. That would give Dirk a shot at hacking into Martin's technology. With the hope for the homecoming of one son, a part of Ellen's conscious self seemed to rouse, and a degree of color returned to her world. Only two more.

Andrew's wife, Celina, and daughter Sylvia arrived bringing more light and life in their wake. Sylvia and Nadie were instant best friends and played joyously together in spite of the language barriers. Uncle Richard had always been a favorite of Sylvia's, and Nadie rarely let him out of her sight; it seemed he always had two small giggling shadows dogging his every step. It complicated the work that Manuel wished to accomplish since his help had increased by two in number, but divided by two in productivity.

Whenever the work for the day seemed too dangerous for little hands and feet, the girls trooped to the kitchen and 'helped' Rosita, or played with Char in the courtyard under Ellen's supervision.   Often, the girls arrived at dinner time ravenously hungry, covered with dirt, and full of new adventure stories.   The adults, on the other hand, while worn out from trying to keep up with their charges boundless energy were provided with distraction from the heaviness of waiting, and with the joy that only innocence can bring. It was a link to reality that kept Ellen from sinking into despair and fear.

Celina, Ellen's daughter-in-law, was a person of sincere, practical faith and being in her presence Ellen felt she didn't always have to be strong. Their relationship had always been good, but now it seemed that Celina was anticipating her every need. She helped Rosita with setting up for the meals, brought Ellen coffee, took care of the guests, and sat with Ellen praying silently in the stillness of the chapel when nothing could stave off the crushing fear and sorrow, and she could only weep and beg God for mercy. It seemed in her Garden of Gethsemane; God had indeed sent her angels to strengthen her for the overwhelming task of surrendering to "thy will be done". While she leaned on Celina's quiet faith, Anna's shared tears were just as healing.

Anna's position with the Apache tribe was extended, and since they were paying her expenses, she was more than happy to remain at the Mission. In fact, if It also appeared that while Ellen had been distant and distracted, Richard and Anna certainly were not, at least not from one another. How could she have failed to notice? Richard excused the amount of time they were spending together saying that Anna was teaching him various dialects which would be helpful when he returned to his research. Ellen often passed them sitting together on the fountain, watching the girls play. Soon they could be found quietly talking after Nadie had gone to bed, in front of the fire in the great room, or reading together in the library. Richard began to get up earlier in the morning ostensibly to take charge of Nadie when her mom left for work. Which also meant they could eat breakfast together.

Nadie decided that if Richard liked to play chess, then she should also. Since Nadie was learning to play, Sylvia must also learn, so Richard found himself the child appointed chess tutor to two four-year-old girls. Of course, the appropriate names of the pieces were much too boring for the girls' imaginations, so they gave the individual pieces the titles they found fitting. Consequently, the horses were

Winchesters. The kings and queens were Richard, Anna, Andrew, and Celina. The castle pieces became the Mission. Understandably, one of the bishops was dubbed Manuel, but strangely enough, the other one was named Dirk which he protested loudly to no avail. Needless to say, the intricacies of teaching were compounded by the need for the girls to correct Richard if he failed to call each piece by its proper name. All of this provided an enormous amount of entertainment for Dirk. He would never admit that he was also paying close attention in hopes of learning some of Richard's secrets.

They had all smirked at Nadie's references to "Daddy Richard", but with each passing day, it seemed more of a possibility. Of all her boys, Richard had always seemed least likely to fall quickly in love. However, she also suspected he would be incredibly loyal and committed to the relationship if he ever did. She only hoped he was not entering the relationship out of a misplaced sense of guilt for what he considered his responsibility in the death of Anna's husband.

Andrew finally arrived, looking jet-lagged, sunburned, and relieved. Sylvia's joy to have her Daddy home was barely contained in her dancing, hugging, and chattering. She even tried to explain in her childish way that Uncle Richard now had a mommy and girl also, causing Richard to blush furiously at what the small girls took for granted. After dinner and a detailed account of his adventures, Andrew, who had nearly fallen asleep in his chair, took his little family off to bed. He had dropped Martin's black bag in Ellen's office, and although she had conversed and enjoyed the evening, it loomed in her consciousness as a specter she must confront.

Nothing that Martin had owned was more closely connected to him. Ironically, the truth was that this dusty leather bag had spent more hours at his side than she had. For a few moments, Ellen sat holding the bag to her aching heart, then piece by piece she emptied the contents examining each item for some particular significance. Andrew was right; he seemed to have taken only the bare necessities. Had Martin expected to return shortly or had he merely wanted to travel light? Still, it was hard to see each item, as if he was out there somewhere with no resources, no comfort, no emergency supplies. He seemed to have left with no backup plan.

Inside one of the zipper pockets, Ellen found a tattered plastic bag. It was the regulation size to hold liquids when going through airport security, but this one did not contain Martin's ever-present hand sanitizer. This one held an old-fashioned wallet photo insert. Dirty plastic sleeves had pictures stuck in them; carried for so long in the heat, moisture, and dirt that they were permanently glued together. Ellen saw that the first picture was of her. It appeared to be her senior high school photo. It must have been the first photo she had ever given him. The face looking out beneath the smudged and dirty plastic was so young and naïve. Ellen sighed; it was a lifetime ago. The rest of the pictures were school photos of the children at various stages of development. Surely, he must have had more recent pictures on his phone. Why did he keep this? Maybe in case his phone was lost or taken; after all, no one would want this. Somehow it was reassuring that he did, but why did he have to leave it behind?

Checking his electronic devices was useless as both were password protected and needed charging. If there was any vital information, it was probably not on either device since Martin had been careful to the point of paranoia. Still, it would be comforting somehow to read his thoughts and notes if Dirk was as good a hacker as he thought he was. When Ellen found Dirk in the great room; he looked up expectantly, almost as if he had been waiting. Was he too eager? What if he had some agenda for wanting this information? Maybe he wasn't a member of some organization, but that certainly would not restrain him from selling information to the highest bidder. Unwittingly Ellen remembered her first impression of him as a pirate.

Reading her body language and perplexed expression, as she clutched the devices tightly to her, Dirk spoke reassuringly, and "I don't do what I do for money Ellen. I do it for the challenge of unlocking a secret, a puzzle. I do it because I can, and others can't; which somehow gives me a rush." He winked conspiratorially then looked away. "And now and then I do it because I like someone, and life has given them a raw deal, and I want to help them settle the score." He spoke the last words with compassionate conviction and looked into her eyes.

She wanted to trust him, but this was the last shred of Martin she had. Then again, if she did not trust him, she would never know what it was that she did have. Sighing in resignation, she set them on the end table next to him. He caught her hand and squeezed it gently. Ellen smiled weakly.

"Here is a list of the passwords he used that I remember. Also, here are birthdays and other relevant dates, I have tried all these unsuccessfully, but there may be a combination I haven't thought of trying."

"This may take me longer, depending on the complexity of the password and the fact that I do not have a server available to run the algorithm." Dirk apologized.

Turning away, she added, "You can use the desk in the library. I can give you my internet access code since it is a faster signal." Returning with the code written on a slip of paper, Ellen failed to add that she, in fact, wanted him to be where she could casually pass by and keep an eye on him. It was a tactic she had often used with her children to monitor their online activities.

Dirk, for all his usual nonsense, became quite serious when he set down to work. Ellen passed by often over the next 24 hours, but he never seemed to leave the desk. He also did not sleep and only ate and drank the food that was placed within reach and even then, did not appear to know or care what he was consuming. When Dirk finally claimed success, he confessed that there were still encrypted files on the laptop that he could not open; these he recommended deleting, but he could give her access to the documents that were on the hard drive. The separate storage device held mainly photos and reference materials. Dirk cautioned that the photos would probably be the most dangerous since those who wanted to find Martin would be most interested in the people and places he was photographing. His camera was both his blessing and his curse. His photos could be used to identify the locations that he visited, but if he did not take the pictures his identity as a "tourist" within restricted countries would be questioned by the local authorities.

For a couple of hours Ellen, Richard, and Andrew sat looking at the ghost and the who, and where he had haunted, at least it seemed so to them. Ironically, the pictures of Martin smiling with children and families cut the sharpest.

"Why did he never seem this happy when he was with us? His own family." Andrew asked sadly. "He never could give up trying to fix us long enough to enjoy being with us."

Ellen did not need to give him an answer; he already had. Only the oldest pictures contained students and others that she recognized. Looking at the historical sites and monuments became a sort of game as they tried to identify what country he was in at the time. Since his camera had always been part of the tourist costume he wore, there were a lot of pictures. He was also often discreetly snapping shots that would not have been sanctioned by the authorities in various sensitive areas if they had been found. Still, he had always been an excellent photographer, and Ellen found herself wishing he was there to explain the stories behind many of the faces. If they could have known these people the way that he did, maybe they could have come closer to understanding why he felt he had to go.

From the pictures, they moved on to the documents. Most were lectures, sermon notes, slide presentations, and outlines. Even with a casual glance through them, one could easily see the themes of Martin's ministry represented.

"Love is to put the needs of another ahead of your own."

"Faith is taking the knowledge you have of God and putting it into action."

"We are the ark of the new covenant containing the spirit of God. When God wants to touch someone, he sends us into their world."

"I have enough time to accomplish all that God wants me to do today."

"The person in front of me is more important than anything I have to do today." Ellen always had liked that one; she just wished that Martin had been able to apply it at home. In fact, these mottos that Martin preached to others were often the very things his family wanted most from him. What he felt needed to be done had nearly always taken precedence over the needs that the rest of the family had.

Richard asked if she would put the sermon notes and outlines on a separate drive for him to look through. He explained that he would never have the insight his father had, but maybe he could learn by studying them. Ellen squeezed his hand. Richard would probably never grasp how much closer he was, with his gentle unselfishness, to practicing the principles Martin had advocated than his father with his driven personality had even been. Andrew moved the photos of buildings and landmarks to a separate storage drive for further investigation. After Ellen had transferred the files for Richard, she would hand the laptop over to Dirk to wipe as clean as possible. She considered smashing it completely, like with a sledgehammer, but for some reason, she couldn't bring herself to do it.

Nadie skipped in and dragging him by the hand insisted that "Daddy Richard" come and feed the silly prairie chicken immediately.

"We're working on that." He muttered referring to the title.

"To bring it about? That sounds great to me!" Andrew teased. Richard shot him a warning glance and left with his little miss who must be obeyed.

"So, what do you think about our confirmed bachelor? Is he going down? Might even end up a dad and a husband all at once." Andrew's joking manner often held a deeper concern.

Ellen sighed. She wished her sons did not have such a struggle to accept the commitment and responsibility of relationships. Their experience with a distant father had left them with a deep desire to either avoid the entire scenario like Richard or to attempt to become all that their father was not. Consequently, the eldest, Andrew had chosen to be a twenty-four/seven accessible stay-at-home dad. Ironically, it was Richard who had the deepest sense of loyalty and protectiveness. He truly would try be a chivalrous knight in shining armor if he did pledge his love to someone; although his expectations for himself would be set so high, he would surely feel he was failing. Somehow, Ellen wished she could convey to her boys that they were not compelled to commit the same sins of omission that their father had.

"She is a wonderful person, Andrew, and she would take good care of him. Or maybe I should say that they would take good care of each other. But I'm not sure it's true love, whatever that is. More like a fulfillment of their mutual sense of responsibility. Anna to find a father for Nadie, and Richard to make amends for the loss of her husband." Ellen explained.

"Still 'taking good care of each other,' is not a bad premise for a successful marriage. After the initial romantic glow wears off, if you don't find ways to take care of each other, it's probably not going to last very long," Andrew added thoughtfully. He laid his hand gently on her shoulder, "We've got to get back in the morning Mom. I'm sorry we can't stay longer till Chris gets back. But Celina has to get back to work, and I've got to meet with the producer to get this documentary together. Will you be all right? This is a lot to handle."

Ellen hugged him to her side. She wanted to be strong, but her words were accompanied by a watery smile, "No worries. I'll be fine. Things need to get back to normal around here so I can pay the bills." She added with a bravado she did not feel.

Andrew had never been easy to fool, but she appreciated him letting it go with assurances that he could be back in a couple of hours if she needed him. Ellen's heart felt too sore for sleep after viewing all the images of Martin, so seemingly alive and well. As if she had leaped to another time and place, and when she returned all her pieces had failed to reassemble properly.

As she transferred document and lecture files to the jump drive for Richard, a file named Quixote's Manifesto caught her attention. Given Martin's affinity for Don Quixote, the title was too intriguing to pass by unnoticed. Ellen read the following:

"Oswald Chambers has challenged us to become a sacramental personality. Like Paul, who "wherever he went Jesus Christ helped Himself to his life." In this manner, Chambers suggests being readily available for God to use in whatever location or to whatever purpose, God would intend. I would probably take this even a step further for to be available for use is not the depth indicated by being indwelt and completely under the control of the Spirit of God. Not only must Christ become incarnated, fully alive within me personally, but also to become fully Christ-like within a culture would then require me to become incarnate, as well.

Not as some emergent thinkers have suggested where one's actions, lifestyle, even political views are substituted for a willingness to speak or to assume the label of a follower of Christ. Rather, I must live as the Spirit of Christ entirely within the cultural framework of the people. Christ became human; perhaps, I should become part of one of these remote tribal groups? If this new breed of terrorists continues their current expansion, the window of opportunity will slam shut. Once they have established their caliphate, the only option for all believers is to flee or to be martyred. Hence, if the option becomes available to enter fully, I must assume it is God's call to incarnate myself even as Christ was willing to do. Perhaps Hudson Taylor was right to divest himself of his western-ness and adopt as much as possible the Chinese culture. He said, "I have but one candle of life to burn and would rather burn it out where people are dying in darkness than in a land that is flooded with light."

There was more to the file, but Ellen considered it pointless to keep reading. No doubt, he must have done exactly that; gone to "incarnate" himself within the tribal cultures. Scanning the rest of the document, she was not surprised that there was no mention whatsoever of the impact such a decision would have on her or his children. Had they ever been anything more than obstacles to his vision of his calling? Once again, and for the thousandth time, she wondered why God had allowed him to marry. Was this to teach her some new level of self-denial? Now those very children, he had so easily disregarded, were out there risking their very lives to find him. It seemed so pointless if this form of ministry was what he wanted, what he had chosen! Why should they even care or bother?

Experience had taught her that if she continued in this vein of thinking, she would soon be overwhelmed with anger and bitterness. It must be wrong for her to judge Martin for his decision. How could she fault him for so noble a desire as reaching these unreached people with the message of God's love? What did it matter the anguish, the loss, the anxiety he inflicted on them in the process? Their lives were not in danger as his was; that is, if he was even still alive. However, he was not the apostle Paul, a single unattached man! Like Peter, he had a wife! Peter said a man ought to live with his wife in an understanding way so that his prayers would not be hindered. Had their marriage vows, made however naively and passionately, meant nothing? Not even to God?

She shook herself mentally. Stop! God was the one who promised never to leave her or forsake her! He never promised that her husband would not, regardless of what his marriage vows had said. She could not blame God! She needed to trust that He was faithful to her, even if Martin in his blind devotion to God had not been. Martin was in God's hands, whatever the outcome was; God would have to decide his culpability. She needed to focus on getting Chris and Stephan home.

Chapter 12

Saying goodbye to Andrew, Celina, and Sylvia was difficult for Ellen but seemed even more so for Nadie. She disappeared after the car pulled away leading to a frantic search of the Mission. Ellen walked into the dimness of the chapel to find her small shadow curled up on the front pew. Her relief was replaced by concern as she saw the loss and sadness of the lonely little figure. Gathering her into her lap, Ellen promised that they would return soon.

"They leave; they not all come back," Nadie spoke in her broken English with tragic certainty. Swallowing the lump in her throat, Ellen replied, "That is true, and when that happens, it hurts a lot, but I think God will help us if we ask Him. Would you like to do that? Is that why you came into the chapel?"

Nadie nodded, pointing at the crucifix, "He knows."

"Yes, he does," Ellen answered, feeling that her faith was so small next to the certainty of this child. They said their prayers and then Ellen carried her back to her anxious mother. With a heavy heart, Ellen returned to her office, resting her aching head on her arms.

Her computer chimed, and a message popped up. It was Chris, and it was what she had been dreading.

"Stephan has not returned from the camp where we were working! He was with another group that had more local workers. Our group has been back for a couple of hours to the operational headquarters here, but he has not reappeared. The Director will not allow us to go back there to see if they are all right, in fact, if they have been taken, we will most likely be evacuated immediately! If that happens, I will wait, as long as possible, but in the end, I won't have any choice!"

"They leave, they not all come back," chimed a small voice in her mind.

Panic seized Ellen's throat; her blood ran cold, and she began to shake. Tears were running down her face as she clutched her sides moaning, "No! Dear God no! Not another one! Please! We've all lost enough!"

Visions of beheadings and crucifixions from the news flashed unbidden through her mind, but this time, every face was Stephan, Chris, or Martin. In the midst of her initial gut-wrenching reaction, she held on with guilty grasping to one ray of hope. At least so far, Chris was still free! She had to face the horror of what Stephan's capture meant, even to deal with her level of responsibility for his being there. Was she accountable? Did he go to try to find Martin because he felt guilty and liable to her? They did not know what had happened to Martin, but they could predict with grave certainty what would probably happen to Stephan based on the reports coming from that area. It seemed so unfair that he should be lost trying to rescue Martin. Although he had committed to make this trip it did not seem like it was Stephan's fault that he was there; it had been Martin's choice, and that choice had drawn in yet another victim.

"Please God, have mercy on him! He did not know what he was doing!" she prayed sincerely echoing Christ's words. Begging God for mercy was all she could do for Stephan now, and imagining his death would help no one and would probably drive her mad. She had to focus on the fact that Chris would surely be evacuated. Her heart ached for her son who now would have to deal with both his sense of failure for not having found his father and for "losing" Stephan. Still, at least he would be safe. Away from the madmen who were so bent on destroying everyone in their path. He had done all that he could do. His western, Caucasian looks and mannerisms meant he would soon become a target if he remained.

Time ground to a halt as they waited to hear more. Fortunately, this was a slow season of the year as far as guests were concerned. The tense dread and fearful hope seemed to hang about them all as the smoke from the fires had hung over the Mission. It choked and threatened to destroy even though did not consist of actual substance. Then finally, Dirk rushed into her office and placed a breaking news story from an online service in front of her. It read, "Dr. Stephan Pierce, a renowned British philanthropist, has reportedly been taken captive while on a fact-finding tour with a noted international NGO. At this time, the British government has not been able to ascertain which group is responsible for his abduction and as no demands have been made, there are also no ongoing negotiations for his release. The NGO will be evacuating their remaining foreign personnel as a precaution."

Ellen wondered then about the letter Stephan had left behind. Maybe she should forward it to his family. She looked at it, lying so official looking in her desk drawer, uncertain what she should do, or even where she should send it. There was no way to know without opening it. When she picked it up, it seemed heavier than she remembered; as if the full weight of its implications could only now be felt. However, opening it constituted a finality, an admission that he too was dead, and she just could not face that. She slid it, unopened, back into the drawer.

Lying beside the envelope when she placed it back in the drawer was the picture she had taken from Chris's room. Was it time to contact her? The girl with the big dark eyes who stared smiling from the old photo. She might still have her email address, as it had always been her policy to become friends with the friends of her children. Her commitment to know them well had been particularly important when Chris was passing through some dark days in high school. As an angry young man who felt he would never be able to measure up to his father's expectation, Chris had relied on his friend group. Ellen, in her way, had also relied on them. They would contact her when he seemed too down, to lost in the darkness, even too self-destructive.

Whatever Chris's faults were, he always managed to find a group of friends who were responsible, caring, and the characteristic he valued most, loyal. Ellen did not know what had happened to Kara since her father had rejected Chris. Possibly by now, she could even be married. If she had married, it was likely less her choice and more her father's choosing. Still, if she had ever cared for Chris, surely now she would be willing to pray. Ellen sent a brief email to the address she had, only detailing where Chris had been working and asking for her prayers that he would be safely evacuated. To her surprise, a response from Kara came almost immediately.

"I am so grateful that you contacted me! You will never know how much it meant to receive your message. I will pray without ceasing for Chris! Please, I beg you to let me know as soon as you have any information or that he is safely home," Her email read.

Chris did finally arrive after long flights and days of debriefing; his haggard, and hollow expression revealing more of the horror he had seen than his words. Like a ghost, he moved among them, silently and sadly, with bits of himself, gradually returning to fill in his form day by day. Nadie adopted him quickly and seemed, with incredible childish sensitivity, to feel his deep pain. Ellen would often find her, sitting quietly beside him with one small arm around him, holding him while tears that he did not even feel rolled down his face. She would smile softly up at Ellen and continue to pat him gently with her other hand. The fellowship of their suffering though silent was beautiful and poignant and Ellen felt that to intrude she would have had to remove her shoes to walk on this holy ground.

Rosita, also, could not let him pass without pulling him into her motherly embrace and holding him close. Usually, she then placed some comforting food in his hands, which he often ate mechanically. They were all eager to hear what had happened but felt that to ask would be to shatter the thin layer of protective ice shielding his soul. His cheeks and body began to fill out as if love and safety were the warmth that was being absorbed into his soul from the outside. Ellen braced herself preparing for the day the ice would crack; would he explode or drain away to nothingness? It was hard to imagine he was the same brash, cocky, confident young man who had left less than a month ago.

The crisis came in the middle of the night; Ellen awoke when Char's whine alerted her to strange sounds coming from the library below her room. Throwing on her robe, and clutching Char's collar she crept silently down the stairs to her office and cracked the door slightly to peer out into the darkness. There was only one lamp glowing near a huddled sobbing figure, but to Ellen's surprise, he was not alone. The feminine figure bending over him with long dark hair indicated that Kara had come. She had arrived after Ellen had gone to bed and Manuel had taken her to Chris immediately at her request. The sight of her had melted the remaining ice that numbed the pain. Littered around him were pictures of Martin he had pulled from the shelves around the room. Kara held him gently as he shook and sobbed in her embrace. Fragments of words dropped from him as he rocked and moaned. From the bits and pieces, Ellen concluded that someone had recognized Martin, but that person had also been taken when Stephan was; which meant that his hope of finding Martin was snatched away as well.

Gradually, he spat out the bits of the horror he had seen. As it has always been with him, it was the plight of the children, starving, traumatized, injured or brutally murdered which haunted his every waking moment and guaranteed him nightmares when he dared to sleep. Finally, he reached the end of his gasping tears and remained curled on the sofa with his head on Kara's lap; chilled, trembling, but empty of the horror. Ellen brought a pillow, covered him with a warm blanket, and brought him some hot tea. When exhaustion finally subdued him, Ellen tried to get Kara to go to bed, but she looked tenderly at his anguished face and said she could not leave him. So, they sat beside him as Ellen had when he was a child overcome by night terrors. Presence, prayer, and love were all that they could offer; only God could bring healing. Throughout the night, they prayed and spoke softly together.

"What made you contact me?" Kara asked in a near whisper as she looked up from where she had been gently smoothing Chris's tousled hair.

Ellen stepped into her office and returned with the picture. She handed it over to Kara explaining, "I found this in his room after he left to go over there, for some reason, I just felt you needed to know."

Kara nodded as tears filled her dark luminous eyes, and said, "I had determined to obey my father when I refused Chris. It seemed the right way to please God by submitting to him. However, I could not bring myself to accept any of the suitors my father picked for me. He would not force me to choose one. He is too honorable to stoop that low, but he thought I would eventually forget Chris and be attracted to them. Finally, he came to me and confessed that he had made a mistake. He realized that I was not just stubborn, but that I had already given my heart away. Only, by now, Chris had stopped contacting me. I was certain that he had given up and that his love for me had grown cold. I prayed to God that if there were any possibility for us to be together, he would send me a sign." Kara stopped, overcome with emotion. Finally lifting shining eyes from the handkerchief in her hand she continued, "Then I got your email. I know that you wrote it, but it was really from God! It was the sign I needed. I am not confident that he still loves me, but I have never stopped loving him. I know he will have many difficult days ahead, but if you allow me to stay, I will remain until he accepts or rejects me."

Ellen could only nod her assent as she reached across from her seat next to the sofa and squeezed Kara's hand while her tears flowed freely.

In the first light, Manuel found them. Looking at the pale gauntness of Chris' sleeping face, he asked softly, "The storm is passed?"

"Yes, I think so," Ellen replied. Gently, Manuel placed his worn hand on the sleeping head and spoke a soft blessing.

Day after day, they waited for any information regarding Stephan. More than once, Ellen held his "to be opened in the event of my death" envelope in her hand and argued with herself regarding what to do with it. It was disconcerting to realize she knew almost nothing about his personal life. Was he married? Did he have a family? Why had he not written an address or given some instructions other than to open it if he died? Maybe she should just send it to the British Embassy?

Even the aid agency that Stephan and Chris had been working with could get no information, and once again, there were no demands for ransom. Chris assumed from all the horror he had seen that Stephan had not survived the week. Reports, coming from the area where Stephan had been captured, dwindled to almost nothing; even the die-hard war correspondents, had to be pulled back from the area due to fighting.

Still, life had to continue, and once again Chris had to process the stages of grief; it was as if he had lost not only Stephan but also his father all over again. At the same time, he could not erase from his memory or psyche all the trauma he had seen. Whenever it all came rushing back, it seemed he tried to run away, to flee if possible, this demon of post-traumatic stress. When he felt the anger overwhelming him, Chris would often take a dirt bike and ride the mountain trails at breakneck speed risking life and limb. It seemed he secretly wanted to die, or maybe, he was just fighting the numbness. The flashbacks continued unabated and the nightmares. He had always been a night owl, but Ellen wondered now if he ever slept. Always, no matter what he was doing or how hard he was running away, Kara was a constant presence by his side.

Ellen could hear their voices from her balcony talking far into the night. Chris sounded so angry and spiteful, yet Kara responded as she always did with gentle love and compassion. The truth was that he did not want to need her; he wanted to fight through this on his own, that seemed the more manly way to handle his stress, loss, and survivor's guilt. Slowly, Chris came to accept his brokenness and to realize how his anger at his helplessness was pushing her away; he started to trust Kara's love and became less fearful and more accepting of his reliance on her.

His recovery was tested when an unmarked black sedan pulled up to the Mission, and three men in suits disembarked. They were the epitome of what Ellen had been dreading. Two of the men were obviously the show of force, and the third was the interrogator. At first, the "Mr. Smith" asked to speak with her privately, but Ellen refused. If he determined to take her into custody, she did not intend to cooperate; he had no charge to bring or reason to detain her. Even if she agreed, there was no way that Richard, Chris, Manuel, and Dirk would let her. The groups faced off with one another across the great room. Her men, Richard sitting on one side and Chris on the other with Dirk and Manuel standing behind them. The two muscle men stood frowning with folded arms behind their spokesman.

At first, they centered their questions around Stephan and their relationship to him; as if they were attempting to find information that could be used to locate and rescue him. Ellen answered was that he had been a guest who became interested in Chris's work and chose to accompany him on his last assignment. Stephan had planned to take the information he found back to the various philanthropic organizations he worked with in the UK. Chris gave them a brief sketch of the day of Stephan's disappearance since there was nothing confidential about that information and not much to tell anyway.

When they asked if Stephan had left a suitcase or any belongings, Ellen felt the weight of Stephan's letter lying in her office and prayed that it would not show on her face. Manuel spared her making a response by answering that Mr. Pierce had taken all his luggage with him since he was uncertain how long his expedition would take. Ellen was thankful that none of them knew about the letter.

Then the questions turned to Martin. Where was he going? What was his occupation? What organization had sent him? Ellen replied that these inquiries seemed irrelevant given that Martin's name was listed among the dead from the plane crash.

Mr. Smith brushed away her explanation dismissively.

"Look, we know you have a photo of him, and since you sent your sons to go look for him; you must have information proving he is not dead." Before Ellen could reply, Chris answered.

"She never sent us anywhere!" Chris snapped back, emphasizing "sent."

"I happen to be employed by the organization I was traveling with and was working while I was there. We have nothing proving my father is alive. In fact, after being there, I am quite sure that he must be dead!" Chris' agitation was growing.

The agent continued directing his questions at Ellen.

"We also know that your other son returned with a briefcase containing a laptop, which we will need to confiscate as part of our investigation."

"Not without some sort of warrant you won't!" contested Dirk hotly.

"Maybe you would like to explain what you are doing here Mr. Watson? What is your interest in Martin Wright?" the agent retorted.

Besides, I'm sure that you, at least, have heard of the Patriot Act, now known as the Freedom Act?" Mr. Smith replied smugly. "It pretty much allows me to take anything I need in the fight against terror." This insinuation was too much for Chris.

"First of all, my father was not a terrorist and would never have supported these jihadist groups! He was a Christian! The only reason he would go to these places, IF he did, was to bring them education and to show them a better way!" Chris was on his feet trembling with rage which caused his voice to shake.

"Furthermore, even if he was alive two years ago, I can guarantee you that he would not be by now! I have seen firsthand what these evil men do to Christians! I have removed the tortured bodies from the crosses where they were crucified! And every time I looked into one of those disfigured faces I was afraid it might be MY FATHER! Do you have any idea what that's like? Do you? No! You don't, because you sit here in your nice clean suits, not bothering to defile yourselves with the horror which you have created!" He dropped to the sofa sobbing.

Kara moved quickly to his side, imploring in her soft voice, "Please, he is not well."

Fearful for her son and alarmed at what else he might unwittingly reveal, Ellen left the room and returned with the laptop. She only hoped that Dirk had managed to wipe it clean enough that Martin's contacts would not be compromised.

Chris jerked to attention and grabbed the laptop as she was handing to the agent.

"No! They don't care about the people who are dying over there! They don't even care about the soldiers they send! They care about nothing but their own power and greed! They sell the weapons to these groups, then when they can't control them, they send in their drones and bomb the civilians to oblivion! Don't give in to them mother! He wasn't a terrorist!" He cried wrenching it from her grip.

Ellen could see the other two men moving toward them. Char faced the advancing men with a deep growl and his hackles raised. Mercifully, acting quickly, Manuel laid one hand on the dog and the other on Chris's arm. Gently, he removed the laptop from his grasp and looking deeply into his face spoke earnestly, "Then give it to them Chris, let them see for themselves."

With a sob, Chris tore from the room with Kara following after him. Ellen took the laptop and handing it to the agent said firmly.

"There you have it, now leave! Apparently, you have had my sons under surveillance and know everything that we know, which is nothing at all. We have very little hope that Mr. Pierce will survive and none whatsoever that Martin has. The only verified proof we have ever had was his name on the list of passengers on the flight that went down two years ago. This laptop was left with his friends before that occurred, not after."

Reluctantly, the dark-suited men turned and started for the door. Ellen could hear the restrained growl rumbling in Char's chest as he followed them. When the doors of the Mission had been shut and barred, Ellen went in search of Chris.

She found he and Kara in the chapel. Chris sat rocking back and forth, clutching his arms to hold himself together, repeating, "He's not a terrorist! I couldn't find him!" like a horribly confused mantra.

"Chris!" Ellen pleaded, "Look at the cross! He knows!" She paused when he lifted his head and continued more softly.

"He knows. He knows where your father is, alive or dead. He knows that you did all that you could do to find him. He knows that your father would never cooperate with ANY terrorist organization! He knows because, in some way that none of the rest of us can understand, He is the reason that your Dad felt like he had to go."

Chris dropped to his knees at the altar raising his hands to the cross, he sobbed.

"Why, why did you make him go? Why couldn't he be here when I needed him so much? I just wanted him to care enough to be part of my life! I tried so hard to find him. I failed him again! Why didn't you let me find him?"

Ellen knelt beside him, wrapping her arms around him she whispered through her tears, "I'm not sure we will ever have all those answers, but I believe that He does understand. He knew loss and pain; he felt abandoned. Christ had to accept God's plan even when it broke his heart. I wish I could carry this load for you; it hurts me so much. But as much as I love you and want to take away this pain, I know the Father loves you more! Leave it all here."

Ellen hugged him tightly and left him there with Kara at his side.

Stepping out into the corridor, she could see Richard sitting on the edge of the fountain in the courtyard holding Nadie. Anna had not yet returned from work, so Nadie had been sent to the kitchen with Rosita when the agents arrived. However, there was no way, even in the kitchen that she could have escaped hearing the loud protests Chris had made during the encounter. She hurried over to Ellen with Richard in tow.

"She is very worried about Chris" Richard explained with fatherly concern. "Do you think he would mind if she went into the chapel? I don't want to traumatize her."

Ellen thought of all the times she had seen Nadie comforting Chris. A child psychologist would surely object to this little one attempting to help a grown man carry his grief and anger. It was too great a burden to bear. However, perhaps the One who said becoming like a little child was the only way to God, maybe He knew best. Ellen and Richard followed Nadie as she hurried with small, purposeful steps into the chapel.

Nadie knelt in front of Chris at the altar, quite unaware that she had taken the position customarily held by the priest. Her round face was just barely over the altar rail. Placing her two little hands on either side of his face she looked into his anguished eyes.

"My daddy is with His Father," she pointed to the cross. "If your daddy is with His Father too, he is ok. If your daddy is lost," she pointed again to the cross, "He will help you find him. Ok?" Forgetting for a moment the age of his small counselor, Chris responded painfully, "But it is impossible; it's just too dangerous to try to find him!"

"Not if He already knows where your daddy is!" She smiled happily into his sad face saying with pure childlike faith, "He knows!"

Chris sighed heavily but smiled at the sweet little face before him kissing her on the forehead. Feeling her mission accomplished, Nadie skipped around the altar to pull Chris' hand until he stood and followed her into the sunshine.

Chapter 13

Later that evening, Chris was sitting with his arm around Kara close beside him while Dirk attempted to play him chess. Rather uncharitably, Ellen wondered if Dirk found it was easier to beat Chris in his distracted, unfocused state than it was to win against Richard. Still, it was better she supposed to keep him at least partially grounded in the present moment. Manuel was strumming his guitar and Rosita had just brought in a tray with mugs of chocolate, everyone seemed lost in their private thoughts processing the events of the day so that they hardly noticed when Richard and Anna entered the room with Nadie bouncing at their heels.

Glancing up, Ellen could see immediately from their faces that something had changed. She raised an eyebrow in question, and Richard reddened instantly. They stood before her where she sat on the sofa petting Char and pretending to watch the chess game. Richard looked even larger than normal next to Anna's barely five feet of height.

"What's up?" Ellen asked, causing the chess players to look up from their game.

"Well, a…" Richard began and nervously took Anna's small hand in his. Somehow, this seemed to give him courage, and he looked down at her and smiled.

"I know this is not great timing, but now that Chris is back, Anna and I are going to return to Canada. Her contract is finished here, and I need to get back to my research. Also, I am going to ask her tribal leaders for permission to marry her. Even though her people, the TsuuT'ina are located close to Calgary it is not that common for there to be intermarriage with white people. She is a respected member of her community, so we want to go about this the right way." he finished his explanation with a shy excitement.

While the rest of them, sat speechless for a moment, Manuel and Rosita, hugged and congratulated them joyfully. Apparently, they had been less distracted and had been paying more attention to the blossoming romance. Chris shook his head as he attempted to focus. He looked at them dumbly, struggling to absorb this new information. Kara was the first to regain her composure, hug them both happily, and join in Nadie's joyful squealing.

"Actually," said Richard sardonically, "there was no way we were keeping anything a secret once Nadie knew!" Nadie giggled and twirled circles around them unable to contain her excitement.

"Nadie," called Chris and she went skipping to join him. He hugged her to his side, and she patted him gently.

"You will be ok? You and your Kara?" she asked in her sweet bird-like voice. Chris nodded sadly.

"Good! You take care of Pheenix!" She said poking him in the chest with her finger, happy that she had managed both the use of English and the bird's name. A faint twinkle returned to Chris's sad eyes, "Doesn't Daddy Richard want to take him with you?" he asked mischievously.

"No!" Nadie shook her head emphatically. "He would not like to live in our land; it is too cold. He would get froze." She placed her small hands on the either side of Chris's face forcing him to look in her eyes.

"You must take care of him." She said and added gravely, "And of your Kara."

"I will do my best," Chris promised seriously taking Kara's hand and looking in her eyes.

Ellen turned to Richard, who stood there beaming with a combination of embarrassment and happiness.

"So, my confirmed bachelor son, care to explain how this happened?" She teased.

"Well, Nadie needs a Dad, and she sort of picked me. Anna didn't call me cute, and she is committed, compassionate, and beautiful. I love them, and I want to take care of them both. Even though I'm a "Dìigúc Dìná", a white man, she still said yes when I asked." He added grinning happily. With a groan, Dirk dramatically slapped his forehead falling limply on the nearest sofa.

"Gah! A woman I forgot to ask!" he moaned loudly. After the laughter had subsided, Richard continued earnestly.

"She has a calling; it's her mission to help fight alcohol and drug abuse among her people. I want to find a way to preserve the wildlife and natural resources. The more we have talked about our perspectives, the more we feel that our missions complement one another. A holistic approach must include the land and the people; they cannot be separated without harming one or the other."

Anna's face glowed with appreciation and maybe even love. Dirk turned and asked Nadie something in her language. She looked at him solemnly and answered him thoughtfully. Anna, the only other one who understood all that she said, wiped a tear from her eye. There would be a ceremony with her tribe and family if they accepted Richard, then they promised to return to the Mission for a chapel wedding in six weeks' time.

There were hugs and tears and laughter as they hurried off to begin their packing. It would be a long journey together back to Canada in Anna's old battered truck, but at least this time she would not have to drive it all alone. As soon as they had left the room, Ellen turned to question Dirk regarding what he had asked Nadie.

"I ask her if she thought they loved each other," Dirk said pensively. "She said her Daddy had loved them by always taking care of her and her mommy, but not himself, and he died. Now Richard wanted to take care of her and her mommy, but this time she, Nadie, would take care of him, and he would not die. I guess that's what she thinks love is, taking care of each other."

"Love is a decision of your will to put the needs of another ahead of your own." Ellen could almost hear Martin's voice as he had said those words so many times. Well, maybe he would be proud of Richard, and his new calling. To Martin, life had to have a higher purpose or meaning. It had never been enough for him, personally, to live a simple ordinary existence; he had to save the world. Maybe if Richard's higher purpose were enmeshed in his taking care of Anna and Nadie, he would avoid the failings of his father. Ellen did not realize she had sighed aloud until everyone looked at her questioningly.

"Sorry, I just heard a ghost." She said.

Later that evening, once they had finally managed to get Nadie calmed down enough to sleep, Anna asked to speak to her privately and led the way into the chapel. For several moments neither of them spoke, just sat together absorbing the dim quietude gazing at the stone crucifix. Finally, Anna confessed humbly, "I must tell you that I do love Richard, but sometimes it feels like that means I'm disloyal to Charlie." She paused looking down at her hands, "It's just that we were so young when we married, and he so quickly became absorbed in his work. It was very important to him, but I often felt set aside." Ellen reached over to hold her hand since she did not trust herself to speak.

"Now with Richard, I see that he feels responsible somehow for keeping Charlie from us, and I worry that he wants to marry me out of guilt. He is such an honorable person that I am afraid it is the only way he feels he can make this right. Charlie and I were married for five years, so I know how difficult marriage can be, and I just don't want to burden Richard with us if he feels guilt, not love."

Her beautiful dark eyes were sincere and filled with tears as she looked imploringly into Ellen's face. It was easy to see how Richard could have fallen in love with her beauty. Her shiny shoulder length, thick black hair, broad smile, and high cheekbones gave her the classic beauty of her people. Ellen smiled reassuringly.

"There is no doubt in my mind that Richard cares for you! You are the first person he has ever shown an interest in romantically. It's hard to imagine him now without Nadie attached to his hand; they have become inseparable. He seems incredibly excited to work with you. But even beyond that, all his life Richard has been drilled with his father's definition of love. It goes like this, 'love is a decision of your will to put the needs of another person ahead of your own needs.' My husband was not very good at applying that precept to his family relationships, but the message is still true. You have been married, so think about it; would that be such a terrible way to live whatever Richard's motivation was for asking you? Especially if you both took that statement as the goal in your relationship to one another."

Anna sat for a long moment staring at the crucifix. Then she turned and grasped both of Ellen's hands saying with conviction, "It is Christ's way, isn't it?"

"Yes, I believe it is," Ellen replied, fully confident now that this was the right woman for her son. Once again God had added the perfect person to her family. At Ellen's suggestion, they knelt at the altar and prayed, consecrating the marriage and the future of the family to God. When they left the chapel arm in arm, Ellen almost felt hopeful.

As brave, as she tried to be it was hard for her to say goodbye to Richard. In so many ways, she had depended on his steady strength. Still, there was no way she would discourage him from this new opening to a life of love. Also, there was the thought of planning a wedding at the Mission, and her mind was filled with anticipation at the prospect. A wedding meant a new beginning and represented a future and hope. However, the hope was bittersweet. Martin would never know Anna and Nadie, even Sylvia he had only seen once or twice, and he probably assumed, as she had, that Kara was already married to someone her father had chosen. Martin was going to miss out on their lives together, and it made her sad. He had already missed so much.

Ellen called Richard into her office for a private goodbye. Throughout her years in ministry with Martin, they had counseled many students and young adults who were in cross-cultural relationships. Growing a healthy marriage was challenging enough without the added layer of cultural misunderstanding that often accompanied them. Ellen expressed her concerns.

"Are you prepared for the cultural differences that will come up? Not only will Anna have an entirely different way of viewing family, conflicts, and faith, but there may also be resentment from her tribe regarding the wrongs they have experienced as a first nation's people group. You, as a young white male can represent both privilege and oppression. Have you talked with Anna about it or discussed how to handle it?" Ellen asked seriously. Richard nodded and replied thoughtfully, "Truthfully, we have no guarantee that she will be able to maintain her place in the tribe if she marries me. There have been problems in the past for women who married white men. I can't do anything about my ethnicity. It will take a long time before people will trust me; I know that. The only thing that I can do is to stay humble and teachable. If they let her remain in the tribe, I can learn so much more from the tribal elders about the interconnectedness of the land, animals, and people than modern scientific methods can discern.

Also, I think if I have learned anything positive from this situation with Dad, it is that God doesn't always call us to minister to those who will appreciate and love us in return. At least in my case, I hope they won't want to kill me. I have learned too that whatever I do, it has to be in partnership with my family. I promise you; I will never leave them to go off and pursue my mission alone." Richard assured her as he hugged Ellen tightly. Her tears fell on his shoulder, but she blessed him in her heart. Even though Ellen knew how much she would miss him, she could release him now to learn how to love his new family and to obey God.

In the days that followed Richard, Anna, and Nadie's departure the Mission seemed so quiet. Chris gradually began to slow his frantic attempts to escape himself. He had never been as helpful or hardworking as Richard had, but steadily Manuel drew him into the daily functioning activities of the Mission. Manuel had a therapeutic way of affirming and motivating that always seemed to bring out the best in others. Soon Chris and Kara were leading the guests on the trail rides and overseeing the mountain bike expeditions. Good food, safety, and exercise helped to restore his physical health, but his inspiration to put forth the effort was solely due to the young woman by his side.

The guests arriving now were often families escaping the growing heat of the desert cities for the fresh mountain air. Still cautious, Ellen watched the guest list carefully and accepted only the most innocuous and least suspicious. The family with a couple of teen boys seemed most interested in being in the media room after dinner, so there were no guests in the great room on the evening when the doorbell rang. Ellen had begun locking the outside entrances whenever her guest had returned for the evening. Fortunately, Chris and Manuel had followed her to the entrance and were able to catch her when she staggered back from the ghostly figure at the door. Stephan, or rather an almost emaciated, skeletal version of him, stood grasping the solid Mission doorpost. Manuel reached out a sturdy hand to support him as he stepped unsteadily into the corridor.

"Stephan, how did you get here; are you hurt?" Ellen cried, finally finding her voice as Manuel nearly carried him to a seat in the library.

"No, no, just weak and so tired." He breathed out sinking with relief into the soft cushions.

"What… How did you…When?" Chris, having found his voice seemed unable to form a sentence.

Ellen saw that his face had also blanched, and he was agitated and breathing rapidly. With effort, Kara persuaded him to sit down and take some deep breaths. Seeing his distress, Stephan reached out grasping Chris's hands, looking into his face with bright, feverish eyes.

"It's ok Chris!" he spoke fervently. "I'm alive! I survived! You did all that you could do in the middle of that hell on earth, which is why I had to get back here as soon as possible." He looked up to meet Ellen's gaze.

"My escape from capture seems to have caused the government more alarm than if I had been killed. Days of exhausting questioning, 'debriefing' for hours; I understand they have Martin's laptop?" he questioned. Ellen nodded, hoping he would not dwell on the subject for Chris' sake.

"Finally, mercifully the British consulate mandated that I be allowed some days to recoup at an undisclosed location, so I came here. I hope I have not complicated things for you." When Ellen assured him they would be fine; his head sank back into the soft leather cushions in obvious relief.

"Now if I might have a cup of Rosita's fabulous chocolate, I might find strength enough to tell the tale."

Chris rushed to the kitchen and returned in record time with a tray of steaming mugs and Rosita. She never stood on ceremony and scooped Stephan into her motherly embrace all the while commenting in alarm at his emaciated condition. She immediately returned to the kitchen determined to make him some miraculous restorative in spite of his protests.

Impatiently, Chris paced wringing his hands while Stephan sipped with evident relief at his steaming mug. Finally, he closed his eyes and said in a soothed voice, "I dreamed of this…Rosita's chocolate…even this room…all of you…when I was chained to the wall…" his voice trailed off as he shuddered and unbidden tears filled his eyes. No one broke the momentary silence; they all felt the horrible significance of his words.

Chris dropped into a chair with his head in his hands as Stephan cleared his throat resolved to continue.

"We were taken not by them, the terrorists, but so that we could be handed over to them. My understanding is that turning over foreign prisoners was a way for smaller fringe groups to prove their allegiance." Stephan winced when he said this.

"But then the military pushed back again before we could be handed over, so we sat for several days chained to a wall. We were barely fed, just enough to keep us alive, beaten, interrogated…I really wanted to die…" Stephan's voice trailed off as the horror returned to choke him.

"The room was dark where we were imprisoned, so before long night and day ran together and I completely lost track of time. At first, I tried to communicate with the others imprisoned with me; I thought I might be able to learn something about Martin. After a couple of beatings, no one would say anything; we were too weak and afraid. Finally, one day a man came into the room. I knew it was daytime from the light that entered when he opened the door. He was dressed like the others, but he had his face covered, and he wore sunglasses. He said something loudly to the guard who ran out of the room."

They were all leaning forward breathlessly as he continued.

"He came over to me and released my chain from the wall and dragged me from the room. I thought my life was surely over, this time, they were going to behead me, but he pushed me into the back seat of a vehicle onto the floor. Then I was even more afraid because I thought I was about to be handed over to the terrorists where I would be tortured first and then killed. Instead, once the vehicle was moving he leaned over me and whispered in my ear in English, 'For neither good nor evil can last forever; and so it follows that as evil has lasted a long time, good must be close at hand'. I tried to turn and see his face, but he held me down. I tried to speak to him, but he wouldn't let me." Stephan raised intensely shining eyes to their faces.

"When the car slammed to a stop, I was shoved, still in chains, out the door and it sped away! I honestly wanted to run after it! I know it had to be Martin! That was a Don Quixote quote!" He was sitting up now animated, his face beaming.

"But he was gone! It all happened so quickly; there was no time." His voice spoke his frustration and agitation. He sat back, his brief shot of adrenaline spent.

"They had dropped me close to a security checkpoint which I somehow managed to stagger toward, but I must have passed out; because everything after that is a blur. I don't think I totally came to my senses until after the three days of American debriefing when the British Council intervened, insisting that I be released before I collapsed. Most of their questions centered on the man who had rescued me, but no matter how much they pressured me, I never told them who I thought it was or that he had spoken to me." He closed his eyes, weak but triumphant, and sank back once again into the cushions. Then he spoke in a weary but confident voice.

"We did not fail Chris…He is still alive…Almighty God only knows how!" this last statement seemed to take all that he had left. Manuel and Dirk leaned over him concerned, but he waved them away weakly.

"Just must rest…"

Ellen sent them to arrange a room and placed a pillow under his head. Before she could return with a blanket, he was asleep. Chris insisted he would sit with him and carefully removing Stephan's shoes stretched his legs out on the sofa and covered him gently. Ellen was concerned that Chris had suffered yet another shock, but Kara whispered that she would be there to watch them both.

Upstairs in her rooms, Ellen prepared for bed but knew she could not sleep. Relief mingled with concern for Stephan. She wondered if there was someone she should contact? Surely the news of his escape would reach the proper people, whoever they were, since the British Council knew he was free. However, the possibility that the man who rescued him was indeed Martin seemed unreal. She paced the room trying to absorb and understand what she had been told.

Was it Martin, or perhaps just someone who he had mentored or spent time teaching? Knowing Martin, he just might have used Don Quixote as an English textbook. Conceivably, if this person had accepted Martin's faith or been influenced enough by him, he could have felt compassion for Stephan, knowing what fate awaited him, and wanted to save him. Maybe that would explain why he did not say anything else. He might not have felt he could communicate well enough in English to explain what was happening.

If it had indeed been Martin, he could have sent them a message, anything. Chiefly, some explanation for why he did not return with Stephan. Maybe he was afraid to be discovered by the military. He might be in so deep that they would have considered him a spy or a traitor. If he did not feel his work was finished, he might not want his identity known. How did he even know that Stephan was there? Stephan had said that he was taken so that he could be handed over to the terrorist group. Did that mean that Martin was embedded, or "incarnate" as he put it, within the group who took Stephan? Had he gone in without knowing that there would be no way to get out?

Despair and confusion gripped Ellen by the throat; she sat down on her bed, feeling ill. It seemed like ever since Stephan had entered the Mission, her world had turned upside down. Now it felt like it was spinning out of control. She sat for a few moments with her head between her legs trying to restore some equilibrium. She wanted to be happy or at least relieved that Martin was not dead, yet she felt so confused, conflicted. What was she supposed to do with this information? If he was alive, he did not come back; she could not bring back him. She could not even contact him. Where did this leave her?

She was not even able to return to what had previously been normal; as if nothing had happened. When Stephen arrived at the Mission, in her mind, Martin had died in a plane crash. She was a widow. Now suddenly, she was not a widow, but she was still alone. Ellen reached for the study Bible Martin had given her. The marker was in the book of James. It had been one of Martin's favorite books to teach. Ellen read until she reached the royal law, "you shall love your neighbor as yourself." That's what James said she would be judged by, the law of liberty; which meant that "judgment is without mercy to one who has shown no mercy. Mercy triumphs over judgment." It was true that she needed the mercy of God. If so, she would have to extend that mercy, without judgment to Martin.

Finally, in desperation, she knelt and burying her face in the covers cried out to God in muffled tears. There was nothing she could do but hand Martin over to God. He was the only one who knew if Martin was still alive. She wanted to believe he was, but that did not mean that she could bring him back. Furthermore, and this was the hard part, she could not make him want to come back.

He belonged to God. She prayed for God to have mercy on him and protect him, ultimately, his life was in God's hands. Finally, when she climbed exhausted into bed, her head was throbbing, but her soul felt more at peace.

Chapter 14

The next morning was Saturday, so after the guests had all checked out, and their rooms had been cleaned, they moved Stephan to his old quarters where they could care for him more adequately. For days, he seemed driven from nightmare to reality, fever to chills, and horror to peace. As Chris had done, the return of his self was gradual and hampered even further by his age and the physical trauma he had endured. Chris and Manuel were his caretakers, with one or the other continually by his side. Fragments of his ordeal were gradually revealed, but there was no further information about whether or not the man who had helped him escape was Martin. There was just no more to tell; however, Stephan never wavered in his certainty that Martin was the man who had rescued him.

A week passed, and guests arrived to occupy Ellen while Stephan gathered strength. Chris came and went from the sick room with trays of food and books from the library. Ellen never invaded the privacy of Stephan's recovery. Each day the look on Chris's face seemed to lighten from grave concern to a more hopeful expression. The obligation he felt to care for Stephan and the distraction from himself, as well as, having someone to process with who understood his experience was aiding Chris in his recovery. At last, Stephan made his way supported by Manuel and Chris, slowly almost painfully to the dining room for dinner. Ellen could see that he had gained some weight, but still seemed incredibly weak. Throughout the dinner, Ellen often found him watching her with eyes that looked unnaturally bright and intense against his pallid skin, and his expression puzzled her. She hoped she had not offended him in some way.

Each day Stephan spent more time out of his room, and in their company. Often, in the course of her day, Ellen found him sitting on the fountain in the sun discussing various flowers and desert plant species with Manuel as he worked in the garden. In the evening, he would be found teaching Dirk the inner workings and strategy of chess, or deep in conversation with Chris and Kara about their future. Marriage counseling, perhaps? Ellen hoped it would be so. With all his interactions, Ellen found it somewhat strange that he never tried to talk to her. In fact, he seemed to be avoiding her.

Finally, on the evening that Stephan informed them he would have to be leaving soon, he asked to speak with Ellen in her office. When he dropped into the chair, he seemed the vague shadow of the man who had once sat there. His eyes were disturbed, and his confident assurance was gone. Physically, he was gaining strength, but now his body bore scars that would fade over time while the trauma within his soul might never fully heal. Stephan Pierce would never be the same. Ellen had a brief flashback of his first visit. So much had changed since then. The fires had come and gone, within and without there were blackened scorched places, yet she and the Mission had survived once again. Her children had come and gone, come to her in her hour of need, and gone out to do their best to find Martin. Now they had returned to their lives to add this new chapter to their history of coping with their father.

Chris and Stephan still had intensive emotional healing to do, but they were alive. She thought that was all that mattered to her. Did it matter if Martin was alive? If he did not intend to return, if her children could rest now knowing that they had done their best to bring him back, if God could fill the emptiness and remove the bitterness she felt when she thought of him; maybe that was enough., She had not spoken in her reverie, just sat absently rubbing Char's ever-present head, and Stephan looked perplexed. By way of distracting him, Ellen pulled his envelope from her desk and handed it to him. She was incredibly relieved that it was still sealed and that she had not given in to either her fear or her curiosity and opened it. Somehow, it did not seem to allay his consternation. To her surprise, Stephan ripped the envelope apart and dropped his face into his hands massaging his temples. It was such an uncharacteristic display of emotion that Ellen was somewhat alarmed.

"What is it, Stephan? Just tell me." She asked genuinely concerned for his fragile condition.

"This letter!" he said waving the torn shreds in agitation, "It was supposed to inform you that you were eligible for the widow's fund that Martin had set up with us. I was coming to tell you that you would be taken care of, at least financially. Now, I don't know; he's not dead Ellen!"

"Maybe he's not dead Stephan, but what difference does it make; IF the man who rescued you was Martin, why didn't he come back with you when he had the opportunity? Why didn't he at least send a message to us?" Ellen felt the pang she always did when she spoke her most painfully private thoughts aloud.

"I think it is safe to assume he is not going to return. As far as the widow's fund goes, give it to someone who needs it. I don't. I am managing financially, and was doing pretty well, letting go of him until all of this happened." Ellen sighed. If only she could speak those words with confident assurance, but even she heard the resignation, as she said them.

"I am incredibly sorry, Ellen! This uncertainty is not the result that I envisioned when I came here! I thought we would discover him and return him to life, or that I could at the very least, provide you with the widow's fund money. Now I find, I am only returning you to a perpetual state of limbo." He spoke in disgust flinging out his hands in frustration at his perceived failure. He dropped his head in anguish unable to meet her eyes. This was not the self-possessed, reserved British philanthropist Ellen had first met.

"Stephan, the truth is that it hurts. It hurts that he has chosen this life over being with me, hurts that God has either allowed him to do this or called him to it, hurts that my granddaughter will never know her grandfather, but what hurts most of all is that he is willing to allow this to continue. If the man who saved you was Martin, he obviously prefers to be dead to us." She paused for a moment unable to speak as her words hung between them. Finally, she sighed heavily and continued, "However, I cannot be his judge, only God who knows the truth can judge his actions. In everyday reality, I am no worse off today than I was the last time you sat in that chair. You and my children returned, traumatized but alive. I think that I have come to a place of acceptance with God. Serenity is accepting what you cannot change, right?" Ellen spoke earnestly, knowing full well that the next few months of processing their experiences would be a challenge for all of them.

When Stephan raised his head, his composure was completely broken, tears were in his eyes, and he spoke hoarsely, "But how can you accept this? Don't you want to find him? Make him come home?"

"Make him?" Ellen sighed heavily. "Even if I could find him again, it is apparent that he doesn't feel any obligation to me. Martin hasn't even attempted to contact me for the past two years. He seems perfectly happy to be dead to me. Apparently, he values what he is doing more than his life with me, or he would find a way to return. He has chosen this. I cannot force him to love me…" her voice trailed off. Mercy, how could she give mercy? Then gaining control of her emotions with determination, she continued.

"In his defense, you saw how desperate the situation was there Stephan! You know that if he has found a way to work in spite of the horror happening, that he would not leave! If you want to help, then find a way to get resources to those desperate people! If you can benefit them, you will be helping him. Somehow, he has managed to survive for the last two years without depending on the financial support that he was receiving from you, so channel that money into the areas where he would have wanted it to go. That seems to me to be the best way to continue his work."

"But what about you?" he responded leaning forward earnestly looking deeply into her eyes.

Ellen did not want anyone seeing the turmoil of her own heart. She stood up and walked to her window, grasping the ironwork with resolution she answered, "I'm ok. They are not. I have the Mission, Manuel and Rosita, my children, my granddaughter even a wedding coming soon. It is more than many people have, in particular, those who are living in that part of the world. No one here is trying to kill us, behead us, threaten, starve, or abuse us, at least not yet. God is with me, and He promises never to leave. Evidently, He expects me to depend on Him, not on my husband. Also, I guess, since God decided not to burn this place to the ground in the fire, He may still have a purpose for the Mission as well. I am learning to be content where I am. I'm okay here, and for me, that is enough."

Ellen spoke with a confident assurance that she did not truly feel, but hoped someday that she would. Maybe that was speaking in faith. She also felt obligated to reassure Stephan or she feared he would never be free of the guilt that he felt for failing her, and Martin. The next day as he prepared to leave, Ellen remembered the anger and bitterness she had felt toward him when he first revealed his role in Martin's work, and realized to her immense relief, that it was gone now. Now, when she invited him to return as part of the family, not as a guest, she saw the tears fill his eyes as he shook her hand stiffly and turned away.

Turning to Kara and Chris, he could no longer maintain his composure. Gripping their hands while the tears flowed freely down his face he pleaded, "Call me! Day or night, anytime, if you ever need anything, or you just need to talk! Remember, if you ever need me, I will come!" He pulled Chris close for just a moment, and Ellen could see that Chris was shaken. Those were the very words he had always longed to hear from his father. Almost shyly, Stephan took Kara's hand, "You are beautiful in every way Kara, and I am so thankful that God in his great mercy has seen fit to return you to Chris. I have never before met someone with such a tender compassionate heart. I know that wherever you go, you will be the hands of Christ to whoever you touch." He spoke the words as one would pronounce a traditional blessing over Kara's humbly bowed head.

Ellen still did not know all that Chris and Stephan had seen and endured, but it had bonded them deeply. Chiefly, she feared, they both felt they had failed in their mission to bring Martin home. Strangely, Ellen did not share their assessment. Maybe he was still alive, but if so, he had not chosen to return. She still had no husband and would have to manage tomorrow and all the days after alone. They were in many ways back where they had started, and yet, they were not nor could they ever again return to the persons they had been before the events of the last few weeks. Their lives would forever be bisected by the before, and the after of their experiences.

After the car taking Stephan to the airport had pulled out of sight past the sentinel pines, Dirk rubbed his hands on his jeans and announced that since all the excitement was dying down, he needed to find some new entertainment. Ellen realized that in spite of his quirky presence, his unique gifts had been invaluable, and she thanked him warmly and sincerely. Still holding the hand, she had extended, Dirk dropped dramatically to one knee.

"Please marry me, so I don't have to leave Rosita's cooking!" he pleaded with an outstretched arm. Ellen shook her head laughing.

He sighed as he rose to his feet but still holding her hand he said seriously, "I will be here if you need me, you know that." Ellen noticed he emphasized the "you" and nodded gratefully, not trusting herself to speak. She thought she saw him brush tears from his eyes as he leaned down to rough up Char's fur and hugged him.

"Take care of her, you old mongrel!"

As if on cue, a squawking bundle of feathers darted between his legs sending him and Char scrambling for safety as it ran laps around the group. Phoenix had apparently come to say goodbye also. Somehow, both dog and man ended up hovering behind Manuel, who was grinning mischievously. He explained that Phoenix's feet had healed, and he deserved the right to run, so it was time to set him free. As he said this, he looked thoughtfully into Ellen's eyes.

Since Dirk indicated that his ride would be coming to pick him up the following morning, for dinner that evening Rosita gave him a feast to remember. Chicken posole with green chili, beef quesadillas, chile rellenos, chicken enchiladas, fresh homemade salsa with chips, refried beans, Spanish rice, roasted corn on the cob, and sopapillas with honey for dessert. Cooking was Rosita's love language, but she rarely received the full benefit of appreciation for her gift. However, it was not so with Dirk; he savored, indulged, praised and seemed to revel in every single delicious mouthful. They all insisted that Rosita sat down and rested while they cleaned up the dishes and the kitchen. When at last they were sipping their chocolate, everyone confessed they had never eaten anything so wonderfully comforting and satisfying. Kara insisted she must have recipes and cooking lessons.

Ellen would always remember that evening with a warm glow. The delicious food and laughter over Dirk's stories of life growing up in a traveling carnival. He seemed such a part of the family now. Not exactly a son, but more like a brother or a cousin. Somehow this realization only served to increase her apprehension when the next day an official looking although unmarked gray sedan arrived to pick up Dirk.

"No worries," he reassured Ellen at her expression of alarm.

"It seems the bad bug I sent to our listening friend has been discovered." He grinned, "Like I said, it's okay; they don't want to arrest me. They want to beg, borrow, or steal it, undoubtedly to use it on their other allies. Hey, let me know when your crazy boys take the plunge. I want to ring the bell at the weddings!"

With trepidation, Ellen said goodbye to their cyber-pirate begging him to keep in touch so that she could know he was all right. The sight of him climbing into the car of those stone-faced agents looked anything but safe to her. She was going to miss his comic relief and his stories.

With each departure, Chris became more restless. Ellen could tell he would not be able to remain inactive much longer. The help he had given around the Mission had served to occupy his body, while with the constancy of Kara's love and care, his soul and spirit were healing. Nevertheless, it was a far cry from the crisis mode of his humanitarian vocation. Finally, Chris received word from his NGO that he was urgently needed for a posting in Southeast Asia working with Rohingya refugees. Rohingya's are the ethnic Muslim minority group living primarily in the Rakhine state of Myanmar. Because they differ from their dominant Buddhist neighbors linguistically, and religiously they are often in conflict. Many Rohingya in desperation to flee the situation have become refugees in neighboring countries where they are also unwelcome. It was to one of these countries that Chris was being sent.

While the situation concerning the Rohingya's was tense and even volatile, Ellen was relieved that it was not a refugee crisis associated with the middle east. As they rushed to pack his essentials, she prayed that he was ready.

Passing through the library, Ellen found Kara sitting alone on the sofa where she had held Chris together in his agony. She was clutching a pillow and crying softly. She looked up sadly at Ellen with tears in her luminous dark eyes, "I guess I was wrong. Not in coming. I know that he needed me to be here. But I must have been wrong that he would love me or want to marry me again. He has moved on, found another passion for his life."

Ellen wanted to scream and shake Chris till his teeth rattled, as her mother used to say! Why in this most important element of his life; why couldn't he for once not act like Martin's clone? She was about to stomp off to find him when Chris brushed past her into the room. He ignored her completely and dropped to his knees in front of Kara.

"How could you even imagine that I would agree to take this posting if you were not able to go with me?" he asked with breathless urgency.

"When I explained to my boss the work that you were doing in India with rehabilitation business projects; well, he can't wait to interview you for a position that will allow us to go together. And baby, if he doesn't hire you; I'm not going anywhere!" he reached out and cupped her face in his hands.

"I love you so much more than my life! Without you, I can't seem to remember that I need to keep breathing. I want us to be married. I mean, will you marry me?"

Kara slipped from the sofa into his waiting arms, and it looked as though the answer was yes. Ellen slipped her old engagement ring from beneath the wedding band she still wore and handed it to Chris.

"Will this do for now; until you can pick out your own?"

Chris would have protested, but Ellen brushed it off.

"I want you to have it. When you find one you like better, you can return it. It belonged to your grandmother originally."

Feeling that she had already intruded too long, she wiped her face intending to slip out. When Chris called out to her, she turned back surprised.

"Mom! Can we make it a double wedding? You know, Richard and Anna, Kara and I, with Nadie and Sylvia as our flower girls? Here in the Mission chapel? Will you ask them?"

Ellen couldn't trust herself to speak, so she nodded, smiling through her tears. So, this was what God meant by bringing beauty from ashes; two beautiful daughters-in-law and precious Nadie as a bonus! All Ellen wanted to do now was to make her way to the chapel, bow at the altar, and thank the one who gave the oil of gladness instead of mourning. Later when Ellen managed to set up a video call with all her children, spouses, and soon to be spouses, they decided that the following Christmas might be the best time for them all to gather at the Mission for the weddings. The weddings would be the Saturday between Christmas and New Year's Day. Coincidentally, the date was the same as Ellen and Martin's wedding day, but she did not draw this to their attention. Finally, there was joy to be shared and plans to be made. By evening Chris and Kara were winding their way through the mountains from the valley to the world beyond.

Suddenly everyone, including the week's guests, was gone. Manuel and Rosita had gone to pick up supplies, and though Ellen knew they would return before the twilight settled over the valley, the solitude seemed complete. As if the only occupants were her soul, Char's faithful shadowing and the Spirit of the Mission. Ellen wandered through the rooms aimlessly, aware that there were tasks she should focus on, but unable to even determine what they were; she finally ended up in the kitchen. Sitting at the table with her coffee, Ellen thought through all that had occurred. All the while they had been caring first for Chris then Stephan, she too had been trying to process her emotions, hurts, and losses. The truth was that the busyness and occupation had been a blessing.

Now that there was no one that she had to be strong for she had no choice but to look inside. Humans, especially women, are relational beings who find it easier often to focus on the needs and emotions of others; however, solitude leaves no one to relate to but oneself and God. Ellen felt that the mantle of her soul was worn, frayed and scorched. Physically and emotionally spent and now alone for the first time in weeks; suddenly having no one to take care of, no guests, children, Stephan, Dirk, and still, no husband; she felt empty. Everyone, but her seemed to be moving on with life.

Suddenly there was a tapping at the kitchen door that led to the courtyard. It was a Dutch door which allowed Ellen to unlatch and open the top to see who was outside. She was surprised when at first she didn't see anyone then when the tapping resumed below her; she looked down. There at the bottom of the door, fluffing out his feathers Phoenix clacked a greeting which sent Char bolting behind the kitchen island. Ellen laughed and retrieving a glove, and some bits of meat held them over the door for the begging bird. Satisfied at last he raced across the courtyard to perch on the fountain for a drink. Ellen considered whether she might need a notice warning, "Do not feed the roadrunner!" to keep her guest fingers safe.

Leaning against the door jamb watching the bird, which could nearly be called the Mission mascot now, the significance of Manuel's words came back to Ellen. Like Phoenix, they had all been through the fire and would forever carry the scars, but they were healing and could run again. It was time now, for each one of them to find their mission. Would her children ever really be free of uncertainty regarding Martin? Perhaps not. Learning to live with the ambiguity, the story with no ending or closure, even to find the ability to forgive would cost some of them more than others.

To Andrew's more secular mind, his father would still be putting his job above his family. That Sylvia would never have a relationship with her grandfather was almost more than Andrew could forgive. Even though Andrew had committed to putting his family before his career, within his own personality, he had to determinedly fight the perfectionism and drivenness that made him most like his father. What he despised he could so easily become. With his high expectations, even God failed to reach his standard of perfection. Ellen prayed that Celina's faith would keep him grounded until he found he could trust the heavenly Father.

Kate would experience it as yet another rejection; if she was not worth her father's time; then she must not matter to him. She believed that she had not measured up to Martin's expectations, and unless or until she could, he would never approve of her. Kate had felt she could never do enough to earn his love or to reach his standards. Now, she would need to find the healing and affirmation of her heavenly father to make up for that loss.

Chris carried the most scars and felt the biggest failure to "reach his full potential" in his father's eyes. He had been thwarted even in this last desperate attempt to prove himself worthy by searching for Martin when, once again, his father was not there. He would also have to live with the guilt of his failure to make contact with Martin, and the faces of the dead in his nightmares would still be his father's. Perhaps, he could find healing through the father-son bond he had developed with Stephan. Ellen hoped they would be able to keep in contact with each other; it seemed vital to both of them.

Richard would continue as he had always done, just to miss Martin. Miss the opportunity to ask his counsel, to understand his passion for his work, to know him. Richard who most wanted all his loved ones to be together would never get to show off his bride and his soon-to-be daughter. There would be no father of the grooms for the weddings. Could they forgive that? Still, God in his mercy had provided loving spouses for each of them; there was healing in being loved in spite of one's scars.

And she, how was she to move forward? Ellen wandered down the corridor toward the chapel lost in her reverie. There was no one there to love her to healing. Although the bond between she and her children was stronger than ever, they still had their separate lives to lead. She could not depend on any human to provide her need for love and companionship. She had only God, and there was only one way to be right in her heart with regards to Martin. She walked to the front of the church and knelt at the altar. Again, she laid her husband at the feet of the only one who could understand. God alone knew if Martin was still alive. Only God could fully understand Martin's calling, his motivation, even what were his responsibilities to her and his children. There was so much that she could neither discern nor comprehend, and she had absolutely no control over what had, or would, become of him.

When Ellen finally stood with Char's help, she felt weak, washed out, but somehow lighter. Her loneliness and all the bitter load of baggage regarding Martin was now laying at the altar at the feet of the Christ. With her heart exposed now to God, she knew she could not stop loving him. God would have to take responsibility for him now; she could not carry it any longer.

Turning from the altar, she stood for a moment looking up at the scripture carved into the massive cross beam. Jeremiah 9:2 "Oh, that I had in the wilderness a lodging place of wayfaring men" It was the goal for which the Mission had been founded, to provide a space for rest. She was now the caretaker of that sacred trust to offer a lodging for wayfarers, the weary travelers of life. As Ellen had discovered, the world outside the Mission walls had become an overwhelming, fear-filled, even threatening place.

The Mission had served its purpose well for her and her children. Its strong arms had held her family together through all the anguish of their experiences. The crucifix, the altar, the pews and even the extinguished candles held a significance that grounded Ellen. She felt her spirit entwined now with each part of the Mission as s a precious or painful link to her memory and her soul. Even admitting the trauma they had endured, her sons, and also Heather and James had found love within the Mission's secure embrace. Surely, Chris and Stephan's recovery proved that the healing power of God's love was here, present and accessible to whoever entered. Her calling was to make available this resting place for the weary to find refuge. Ellen had found her mission.

HISTRIA BOOKS

HISTRIA CHRISTIAN

Other fine books available from Histria Fiction:

For these and many other great books visit
HistriaBooks.com